Silver's Revenge

This is the sequel to Robert Louis Stevenson's *Treasure Island*, and is a light-hearted and affectionate account of the pirates fifteen years on.

Tom Carter tells the tale at the request of the crew who had settled on Treasure Island for good and, taking no chances, he stows the story in a rum cask and floats it off on the north-east current to reach our shores. Thus, the intention of the pirates to 'entertain and instruct folks, when and if we return to Old England' is fulfilled.

Robert Leeson

Silver's Revenge

Lions

First published in Great Britain by
William Collins Sons & Co. Ltd 1978
First published in Lions 1985
Second impression January 1990

Lions is an imprint of
the Children's Division, part of
the Collins Publishing Group,
8 Grafton Street, London W1X 3LA

Printed and bound in Great Britain by
William Collins Sons & Co. Ltd, Glasgow

Contents

Part Three MY SEA ADVENTURE

Part Four MY SHORE ADVENTURE

For Fred, who knows the island well

Dr Livesey, Master Hawkins, Captain Gray and the others asked me to set down the particulars of our coming here. They say it will entertain and instruct folks, when, and if, we return to Old England.

Squire Trelawney has nought to say on the subject. He's said little since we landed, save to beg my pardon for nigh killing me. Granted, I told him. If he'd done it, I couldn't have taken offence, so it would be overdoing things to complain because he failed.

Mr Argent (that's the name I know him best by) has more on his conscience, wherever he keeps that. His mind's busy with the bar silver. But how to get it without going too close to the people up at Spy Glass Hill, there's the rub.

Ben Gunn is happy hunting goats round the island, but not at North Inlet. He doesn't go near there. To tell truth no one dares go there and I don't blame 'em either.

I'm the only one who has the free run of the island. Who am I? Well, my name is Tom Carter, and . . .

PART

— I —

The Runaway

— I —

The Old Undertaker

My life started with a funeral, and might have ended there too, and no one any the wiser, or sadder, me included, if it hadn't been for Master Oakleigh, the old undertaker.

They called him that day to the workhouse in the town of ——— in the West Country. A poor woman (rest her soul) had died in childbirth. The father (the Devil will take care of him) was nowhere to be found. Her baby had died too, it seemed. And why not? Life was no bargain. So they called in Master Oakleigh to measure the body for the coffin. True it was only a poor woman and a plank box, but he was a craftsman and did his job with care.

So, when he found her lying there on an outhouse bench, her child clutched to her breast, he lifted the baby aside a moment to arrange her rags more decently.

And discovered, to his pleasure, not surprise for you cannot surprise an undertaker, that the child was not dead.

So, by chance my life had begun. Instead of spending my early years (and my late ones) in a box underground, I spent them in Master Oakleigh's house, growing up with his granddaughter, Tilly. He cared for us equally, though he could not treat us so because his son, Young Oakleigh, was as jealous and mean as his father was open and generous. More of that in a while.

Thus I quickly learned what to me is the rule of life. It's a game where good fortune and bad follow one another. Win or lose, at the end of the game, Death takes cards, stake and all off the table, and off you go to your long home, as it says in the Book.

From the time I could walk I was in the workshop. There was a deal of sawing, banging, chiselling, pegging and nailing going on, but with all the toil it was a merry place. As soon as I could totter down the road to the Fox and Grapes with the great jug in my hand, my job was to bring in the ale, without which no craftsman could work.

Don't think Master Oakleigh and his journeymen were tipplers. Not at all, they drank only in season and on occasion, and always by rule. The rules were many and the occasions ever present. If a man struck his thumb with a mallet and cursed his Maker (who guides our hands in everything), John, the oldest journeyman, would tap on the holdfast with a chisel. All would cease work and value the oath, say at sixpence or a shilling, according to its strength, and according to their thirst. And lest the punishment cause bitterness, why the offence was purged right away. Off I went to the Fox and Grapes with the sixpence or shilling, bringing back the frothing jug to restore all to good humour.

If two men quarrelled, one had only to strike the holdfast and the others formed a jury, assessed the difference, or the insult, passed judgement, collected the fine, and off went Tom down the road with the jug. Little Tom they called me, for I was, and I never outgrew the name.

Birthdays, Saints' Days, Quarter Days, all were marked in their turn and in the same way. And it goes without saying that no one went to his long home without a parting salute. The mallets thumped, the chisels sliced, the saws rasped and the jug passed round. And when the work grew heavy, Master Oakleigh would clear his throat and strike up, while others harmonized.

"All people that on earth do dwell . . ."

If the work went flying, John would give us:

"A maid again I never shall be
Till apples grow on an orange tree."

There was a deal of talk, too, of timber and tools, of old ways and new, and much of life and death, about which they knew all there was to be known. As the last polish was laid on a fine coffin with its brass hands and satin lining, Master Oakleigh would place his hand on it and recite:

"Sceptre and crown, must tumble down
And in the dust be equal made,
With the poor, crooked scythe and spade."

Which was, he said, true as far as it went. But men were not equal even in death. Some went into the ground in pine, some in the finest mahogany. But, if care counted, then all were equal. Said Master Oakleigh: "Bury the rich with ceremony, for that is what they have paid for. Bury the poor with dignity, for that is every creature's birthright." Sometimes for a pauper burial there were, aside from the gravediggers, but three at the graveside, Master Oakleigh, the poor curate, whom he had paid, and myself. We would stand there in hot sun, or drizzling rain, gale or snow till the coffin was covered over. Then, when I was very small, the old undertaker would set me on his shoulders and carry me home, taking care always to set me down when we reached the gate for fear Young Oakleigh should see.

As I grew, he found me work to do. I would memorize the names of mourners for the news sheet in Bridgwater, open the doors of carriages, straighten the garlands when the wind blew them from the graves, and when the price was right, dress all in black to act as mute. And at the funeral feast afterwards, I would sing a sad song in a piping voice. For this I was much in demand; being an orphan made it more touching and many a kiss I had from the ladies,

13

dressed demurely in black. Some kissed demurely too, with lips puckered up, some with their mouths open as if I were a mince pie. But all kisses were equally welcome. So, too, was the food, rough or fine, at low funerals or high. I found a taste for wine and delicate meats as well as strong ale and coarse fare.

Thus, when I grew to be thirteen, though I could neither read nor write and had but one suit to my name (my mute's garb of black with its frilled white shirt was put away carefully after each funeral) I had the taste of a gourmet for wine and food, an addiction to kissing and a philosophy on life and death to suit one two or three times my age.

Such a creature must excite some disagreeable attention. I had one enemy from the start, Young Oakleigh, Tilly's father. Not that I worried over much about him, for Master Oakleigh looked after me well. He planned to apprentice me at fourteen.

He seemed set to teach me all he knew, which pleased Young Oakleigh even less. But then my fortune changed. The old undertaker died. He was buried with ceremony for he was far from poor. But the crowds that came from near and far, not least the sober-clad masters and journeymen of the Undertakers' Company who bore his coffin to the church, with his tools laid on top, were truly sorry to see him go.

None more so than I. My observation of life's game taught me that my next hand would be a bad one.

— 2 —

A Fatal Blow

Master Oakleigh knew his son well. So in his will he laid down that I was to be apprenticed and taught the trade. Young Oakleigh had to obey, or lose his reputation in his own workshop, or any other workshop in the county. But he put off signing the indentures as long as he could, and what little he taught me was done unwillingly.

In the short while I stayed with him I learned, in fact, only two things – how to lie to keep out of trouble, how to dodge it when it came. He taught me with the flat of his hand, his knuckles or a yardstick, or ought else that came into his grasp. I soon found it served little to appeal to his sense of justice, for he had none. Instead I learned to judge the changes in his face, like the clouds in the sky. A certain darkening of the features, a knitting of the muscles between the eyes and my limbs would tighten like a spring. I would duck and weave, sidestep and leap, shouting out whether he struck me or not. His anger made him more stupid and the more I roared the better he liked it.

Now and then, though, even the nimblest foot is not quick enough. He would corner his quarry and beat the senses out of me. In agony, I wept silently and my master, missing the rewarding cries, would lay on till his arm fell tired. After one such beating drew blood, the journeymen went to the Company Master and laid a complaint. The Court of Assistants had Young Oakleigh up before them and heard both sides of the matter. They gravely told him that if he apprenticed me he might beat me – that was laid down in the

15

indentures. But he must do it "reasonably" they said and with that they, and Young Oakleigh, went off to dinner.

But after that my master left me alone for a while. He did not seem to want to see me. Which was just as well because at that time, my fortune took a turn for the better, and it was better he did not know about that.

In the summer Little Tilly, who was about my age, had begun to teach me to read, which she herself learned at the dame school.

We had but two books between us. One was *Miss Susan's Sampler*, a little volume of good advice to a young lady. The other was a tattered copy of the Newgate Calendar owned by one of the journeymen. Thus we had good counsel on what we ought to do and ample warning of what would happen if we did not do it. Though, to judge from the Calendar, which we read much more than the *Sampler*, good manners did not always save you from the gallows.

On quiet afternoons, before the evening meal, we would seat ourselves on the staircase which went up to the loft over the workshop, hidden behind the timber stacks. Crouched together in the dusk we would pore over the letters, which I learned quickly, and later read to one another. Sometimes, tired of reading, we would sit arms round each other and talk of what we might be when we grew up. She was to be a fine lady and ride in the Lord Mayor's Coach. I was to be a master undertaker and bury the rich and famous.

Tired of dreaming we would turn to play, to counting and guessing games, using our fingers which in the half darkness we felt rather than saw. After that we would tickle and pinch one another till our gasps and giggles caused Old John to come to the foot of the stairs shaking a warning finger and winking a brotherly eye.

So, with little attention from the father and much attention from the daughter, I thrived. The store of pennies and fourpenny pieces slipped into my fingers at funerals and hidden in a silk handkerchief, all I had from my mother, were turned into a single gold coin for me by one of the men. With all these things I did so well I might have known it could not last.

Tilly and I became careless. One hot day after a funeral which was attended by the men in the workshop, I came back all dressed in my black velvet and white frills, my head a little lighter than the rest of my body from the fumes of a superior Madeira drunk after the burial.

I found Tilly home from school, listless with heat and boredom. We had no books to read but we went straight to the staircase and made ourselves comfortable. Tilly mocked me about my funeral jacket which she unfastened the better to tickle my ribs. Tickling led to wrestling and finding our faces together and her sweat-beaded lips against mine, I kissed her. We strained and struggled together there, gasps and giggles rising in the silence of the old building, with the smell of wood shavings and varnish all around us. I can remember that state of bliss as if it were yesterday.

After a good hand of cards, a bad one. I was seized by my waist band and jerked in the air, then set down roughly on the workshop floor. I could just make out the features of Young Oakleigh and behind him, stock still, stood Old John and the other journeymen.

Tucking my shirt into my breeches as I struggled up from the dusty floor, I said, foolishly, "Miss Tilly's learning me to read."

"It's not what she's learning you, but what you're learning her," came the answer as he marched me to the bench. He turned to the journeymen and said calmly, "I shall beat him 'reasonably' till I see the colour of his blood. Now get out all of you."

With that he strapped me to a trestle, took a rope from the tool box and laid into me. The first to suffer was my fine black suit which sprang into ribbons; next my frilled shirt and last of all my precious skin and the flesh it covered so smoothly.

I might have borne it all, even the blood that streamed over my buttocks, but in one swinging blow the rope end flicked my eye, half blinding me and sending pain through me like a knife blade. My flailing hands struck the top of the bench, my fingers gripped a heavy mallet and with a jerk I hurled it back and upwards.

As he bent to his work it struck him fairly on the temple. I heard him fall to the floor and my workmates rushed in. John unstrapped me.

"Can'st stand, lad?"

"Aye."

He bent to my ear.

"Then run for it, Tom."

"Run?"

"Aye, I doubt you've done for master. Run for your life, lad."

━━ 3 ━━
The Black Coachman

I ran for it – out of the workshop, down the lane at the back
and into the country. As I ran, Old John threw over my
shoulders an old canvas jacket such as sailors wear. It hung
down to my knees and hid the tattered funeral finery and the
still bleeding stripes on my back. As I ran, I kicked off my
fine shoes with their silver buckles. They looked well but
pinched my toes. I was bound for no funeral, not if I could
help it, most certainly not my own. I'd been near buried once
in my short life and had no urge to try it again.

Before I thought of where I might be bound I was two
miles from Oakleigh's and half way along the road to Bridgwater. Now all was dark around me and the farms I passed
showed small lantern lights like stars in the black between
earth and heaven. The road was dust-dry but rutted from
the trundling of waggons. I tripped and stumbled as tiredness
took hold and soon slowed down to a walk. Now I stopped
and listened. The silence was as deep as the dark. If they
were chasing me, they were well behind.

I turned aside, trudged over a pasture and found myself a
resting place at the foot of a haystack. The condemned sleep
sound, and I slept like a man due to be hanged, as I had no
doubt I was. Though I still hoped to put off the business for
a while yet. The game was going badly but I was in no
hurry for the table to be cleared.

I woke when the dawn showed white over the woods.
My back was a-fire, my empty belly churned. But I got on the
road and made what speed I could. Bridgwater stands on

the coach road from Exeter to Bristol, both ports jam-
packed with ships bound for all points of the compass. If
they didn't hang me, they'd transport me. I'd forestall them
and take leave of Old England as soon as I might. Wherever
I sailed, I opined, people died and needed coffins. Not that
I was a fully-fledged coffin maker, not by seven years.
But I was handy with a broom or an ale-jug. I could look
solemn in black velvet or sing sweetly at the feast.

I put on more pace and came into Bridgwater market
place as the mail drew in. With no more delay I sprang up by
the coachman's side as he reined in the horses. He took one
look at my filthy tear-smudged mug, my canvas jacket and
my shredded black stockings and made to push me into the
road again. But I flashed my precious half guinea at him.
He took it without a blink and told me to be back in an hour
and he'd take me to Bristol. I started to ask him what
change I might get of half a guinea, but he scowled at me
in a way that made me think so suddenly of Young Oakleigh
that I fell back from the top of the coach and was lucky to
land on both feet.

I made time pass by wandering round the town, which
was not wise. I soon knew I was being watched and, squinting
over my shoulder, sure enough I glimpsed two men strolling
along behind me. One pointed. I turned left down an alley
and hid in a doorway. They turned into the same opening.
It was too pat for chance. Not seeing me at first, they
quickened their step and rushed past where I hid. I gave
them no second view of me but nipped sharply to the road
and ran back to the inn in the market place. The coach was
in no way ready to go, so any hopes of hiding in the baggage
they were piling on the roof were out. I ducked behind a
corner and waited. My followers came back at a smart trot
and stood looking about them. I made myself smaller in
the shadow and one of them put his head inside the inn door

and called for ale. When the pot-boy brought it, I heard one
ask him.

"Have you seen a boy round here – a scarecrow look to
him, old jacket and black stockings?"

"One such was round the coach just now waiting to get to
Bristol. Who wants him?"

"Justice, my lad. He's half killed his master and run away.
He's for the hemp jig or, if he's lucky, for Virginia."

"Justice, my backside," jeered the pot-boy. "You're after
a reward for turning him in. You're bounty hunters. Damn
me if I'd sell a lad for gallows meat."

One of the men pushed something into the pot-boy's
hand. His manner changed.

"Thank ye, sir. Why I do recall I saw him go towards the
river, that way."

As the two made off, the pot-boy said, over his shoulder,
"Hey, you round the corner. Best run for it. I know you're
there."

"I've paid my coach to Bristol," I whispered back.

"Then it's Bristol Newgate for you if you set foot on that
coach, friend. Go round the back and head west. They'll
never think to follow that way. Hold a while."

He ran back in the inn and came back with half a loaf
which he put in my hands.

"Good luck to you."

"Why d'you help me?"

"Why, 'twill be a better world when all masters are
knocked on the head. Now, run."

I did. An hour later I was hiding under a hedge west of the
town, filling my belly with new-baked bread. I was so hungry
I finished it all in a dozen bites. More fool me. It was the last
good meal I had for nearly a week. That afternoon, though,
leaving the roads and heading over the fields where the grass
was gentle to my near bare feet, I made good time. That

night I slept in the open for the air was warm and the sky full of stars. I dreamt of Old Oakleigh and Little Tilly and just when I had my arms round her I woke up with the dew on me, hugging my arms to myself, my back smarting where the rags stuck to it, and no Tilly to be seen. My head whirled round as I got to my feet.

I took my breakfast from a field of turnips which, for a lad with a delicate palate like mine, lay heavy on the guts. I brooded as I chewed. One moment I was an apprentice (or nearly so) with half a guinea in gold in my handkerchief and the lips of my master's daughter on mine, the next I was a barefoot runaway, his belly full of turnip, and his neck ready for stretching at the next assizes. I set off again before my eyes could start to pipe.

How far I'd gone I could not say, but I knew from the sun I was still heading west. I passed few farms and kept clear of them for fear of their dogs. With my innards creaking and my head dizzy from hunger I went on, only seeking to put as many miles between my body and the bounty hunters who were after it.

Towards evening one day, I struck rising ground. Soon I was in sheep country and climbing into lands where the snipe and curlew were in charge. I saw no one and slept that night in a broken stone hut. Next day the mist was down and I did not dare move for I knew neither east, west, north nor south. But another day of cold and hunger forced me out and I blundered on, tripping on hummocks, rolling in gullies and once walking into a slough up to my knees.

But my luck was not out yet. Around noon, the mist cleared. But I was still near the hut. I'd wandered in a circle. I knew I had to get off the moors before I perished. South and west lay more heath and bogland. East lay Bridgwater and the body snatchers. North, if I was not mistaken, lay the sea. I'd no choice. I headed seawards as fast as I could while light lasted, warmed a little by the sun, the mud crusting on my legs and my guts grumbling at me. My head was in a fever from the pain in my unhealed back and my weariness and hunger. I began to see cottages on the skyline that vanished as I ran towards them, then figures I knew, Old John and Tilly, who smiled and beckoned, then skipped away and left me stumbling alone.

In the twilight, half daft with my empty belly and fevered head I reached a rough road that ran east-west. I turned into the setting sun, the last thinking action I took that day, and tottered on with its rays full in my eyes, till my skull seemed full of its red light. Then, as its last gleam began to slip away, I saw a great vision on the skyline.

On the road before me appeared a coach, a great gilded affair with four prancing dark horses. On the box, swinging his whip, sat a giant coachman in blue cloak and braided hat.

His face beneath it was black as the team he drove, or as the Prince of Darkness himself. In terror I ran like a headless chicken across the road. The shaft head caught me a sliding blow on my shoulder-blade.

Down I went and the whole scene vanished from my eyes.

— 4 —

Life After Death

I half opened my eyes and looked straight into Old Nick's face. He held me in his arms. I'm a goner, I thought. He's taking me for murdering young Master Oakleigh. But I was too weak to struggle and he held me gently. So I lay still and waited for him to sprout his huge wings and bear me off. He spoke some words, deep like an organ note, though I could not make out what they were.

"Hand the boy up, Daniel," someone spoke from above us, very cool and dry. Ah, so it wasn't Old Nick that had me, but only an understrapper. My eyes opened wider and I saw behind him the shape of the coach with its door open. A face peered out, as far as I could see, shrewd and kind, with bright black eyes beneath a white wig. The wig tipped to one side and I saw close-cropped grey hair. Aha, I thought, my luck's turned again. It's not hell I'm bound for, but the other place.

The Archangel Gabriel, or maybe it was St Peter, helped me into the coach. Saint Daniel climbed back on the driving seat and whipped up the horses. Off we went, not up in the air, but along the road. It was a marvel. Did they have a coach delivery for every mortal soul, or was I a special case? White-wig studied me closely, leaning towards me as we swayed along. I could barely see his face in the dusk. But the coach was well-sprung and upholstered and I was comfortable. Then I saw he was holding out a snuff-box. I shook my head. He smiled.

"Come now. I can see you're hungry. It's not snuff. I

24

never take it. It's cheese made in Italy, very nutritious. Try some, I can see you're hungry." I put my head to the box and sniffed.

"Ah, Parmesan," I said. "Better for cooking." Then I blushed at my impudence. But he laughed.

"Why, what a lad. A gourmet in rags." And he slapped me on the shoulder. The pain went right through to my belly. I shied like a colt. He turned, banged with his fist on the roof and the coach stopped. Without giving me time to think, White-wig had my canvas jacket off my back and was peering at my back, probing it with his fingers.

"Steady, lad. What villain gave you this beating?"

I started to answer, but something told me this might not be Gabriel or St Peter after all.

"Come now, lad, you can tell me. My name's Livesey, Dr Livesey. I'm not a doctor only. I'm a magistrate. Just give me the rascal's name and I'll take effectual means to have him routed out and hunted down."

Whoa, I thought. I might tell an archangel I was a runaway who had done for his master, but not a magistrate, even a kind one with a snuff-box full of Parmesan. At such moments, silence is golden. I did the best I could. Closed my eyes and slipped sideways on my seat as if in a dead faint. The Doctor wasted no more words, but tapped again and off we went once more. There was soon no need for deception. The rolling of the coach, the soft leather seat, the mild air all worked together to put me to sleep.

I never felt the coach stop, nor Daniel take me in his arms, but woke up when he set me down again. Warmth beat on my face from a big fire. I was on a bench in a large kitchen. By the range, hands on hips, stood a cook, plump and squat, as black as Daniel, and a young cove in footman's gear, black likewise. I'd heard of such households before, where they had blackamoors bought in Bristol, or shipped over from Jamaica or Barbados. But few of the fine houses I'd been in had such prizes. This must be a wealthy man. Though this Dr Livesey did not have the look of a rich man to me. There was something too brisk and business-like about him for that.

"What do they call you?" the cook asked me.

No harm in telling that. "Tom," I answered.

"Well, Tom, Squire says I got to feed you, while Betsy brings something for your back." She put a wooden bowl on my knee, gave me a spoon and I set to. The first mouthful, mutton and vegetables, was so hot I could have shouted, if my mouth hadn't been so full. Pain didn't stop me though. I gulped it down and sent some more to follow. In a trice I'd finished.

Just as quickly, she took the bowl and filled it up. I ate the next more slowly and tasted it more.

"Thyme and marjoram."

She burst out laughing and slapped her leg. The footman grinned.

"You a kitchen boy, Tom?"

"No – " I started, and stopped before the word "undertaker" passed my lips.

Someone had entered the kitchen behind me while I ate and began briskly but gently to soak off the rags from my back with a warm wet cloth. I put down my bowl and sneaked a look over my shoulder, caught a glimpse of a brown face and snub nose, before a pair of strong fingers took my nose and put my head to the front again.

"Be still, Mr Nosey," said a girl's voice. So I sat still while Betsy finished her work, put ointment on my bruises and went out again. A moment later a clean shirt was pushed over my head.

"Squire wants to see you. Come."

I hastened to push the shirt tails into my breeches which, though dirty, were at least in one piece, and followed Betsy. She was tall and dressed in a long white gown tucked in at the waist and flaring out round her hips. She had a swift swaying walk and did not look to see if I followed her. She led the way down a matted passage and pushed me into an open doorway. It was a great library all lined with bookcases and busts on the top of them. As the door closed behind me I saw Dr Livesey sitting by a bright fire, pipe in hand and white wig on his knee.

"Well, Squire, here's our young gourmet, fed and physicked. Are you better, sir?" he asked me.

I nodded, thinking it best to say nought and looked about me. On the other side of the fire sat a huge man, six feet high and broad in proportion, or one might say, fat in proportion. His face, red-roughened and lined as from long travels was a touch purplish. His hair showed grey under his wig and his white eyebrows bristled as though to show quick and high temper. One cause of high temper was plain to see – the glass of port at his left side and the swollen bandaged leg which rested on a cushion.

"Come here," he commanded. I wasted no time. "What's your name?"

"Tom Carter, sir."

"Where from?"

"From – "

"Where's that?"

"East of Bridgwater, sir?"

"Hm!" he growled as though that were the end of the earth. He beckoned me closer. "So you're a gourmet are you?"

"Doctor's joke, sir," I said respectfully. He held out his glass.

"What do you think of that?"

I sniffed the wine. "Good, sir, and old." Then my eyes fell on his leg and the words slipped out. "Too old for your good, sir."

The Squire's face turned more purple. From the other side

of the fire, came a snort and a snapping sound as the Doctor broke his pipe.

"You may laugh, Livesey, and take your impudent jackanapes away with you."

"I beg your pardon, sir," I began, hurriedly backing to the door, but the Doctor stopped me.

"Serve you right, Trelawney. The lad spoke the truth. Perhaps that's why his last master beat him so hard."

The Squire harrumphed and growled, but finally let himself be talked back into a good humour.

"Well, Tom Carter, do you know ale as well as you know port and cheese?"

"I hope so, sir," I answered.

"And would you like employment?"

I nodded. The Squire glared at me. "You're not a runaway apprentice are you, boy?"

"No, sir," I answered, which was as near truth as I could stray, since though a runaway, I was no apprentice.

"Well then. There's a job to hand for a lad of your skills. Do you know hereabouts – the Admiral Benbow Inn?"

I'd begun to answer, but hardly had my mouth open when our conversation was violently interrupted.

The door was flung open and a young lady rushed into the room.

5

Enter Lady Alice

As the young lady stormed in, the Doctor clapped his wig on his head, sideways, and stood up.

"Lady Alice . . . a pleasure . . ."

But he got no reward for his courtesy, not even a glance. The Squire had all her attention, not that he welcomed it. He shrank into himself, all six foot of him, with a sickly grin on his face.

"Alice . . . ?"

"I will not have it," she said.

The Squire's mouth opened. The Doctor sat down.

"It's monstrous."

I had backed off from the fireplace before she entered and, since she never gave me a glance, could look her over unobserved. Slender, and handsome dressed in black, a French gown with narrow waist, low-cut bodice and lace fichus, a fashionable young widow. I'd seen such before – though always in sorrow, never in anger. Her eyes sparkled. I waited and watched. More excitement was to come.

"Alice, my . . ."

He got no further.

"You said, you said it distinctly, that Betsy was my personal maid. Now I find her being used for all sorts, so she's not there when I call her."

"All sorts?"

"Aye, in the kitchen, washing some urchin the Doctor picked up on the road."

29

I stepped back into the corner, well out of the candle-light.

"But Alice, be reasonable" (fine hope had he), "when we have so few folk in the house, all must bear a hand.

"Besides," went on the Squire, a touch peevish now, "don't forget – I bought Betsy myself."

The Lady Alice plucked out a small handkerchief from her lace and pressed it to her eyes. The Squire's face creased in gloom. "How like you to reproach me with my poverty. And my poor husband not long . . ." Faint snuffling sounds came from behind the cambric and the Doctor rose putting out a hand.

Down came the handkerchief.

"If he were alive, I should not have to put up with such – such degradation." She paused. "Anyway, Betsy was a bargain got for you by that rogue of an agent, Blandly, up in Bristol."

"Aye," said the Squire warmly, "and a bargain she is, always ready to give a hand's turn. Not fifteen yet, but able and willing to serve at all the house needs."

"Aye, too willing for everything but my service." Lady Alice paced aside a step or two and I dodged out of her line of vision.

"It's not to be borne. This house run by a cook, a maid, a footman, a gardener, a coachman and a drunken gate keeper, and I must attend the pleasure of a ragamuffin for my needs."

"You know how tight we're strapped for funds, Alice, my dear," wheedled the Squire. "Not for long, though, I trust. I've a venture or two in mind."

The Doctor looked across the fireplace in surprise.

"Mustn't say more . . ."

Nor did he.

"Ventures," snorted Lady Alice. "All you do is talk of ventures. There's been nothing but talk since that voyage fifteen years ago with the Doctor and – Master Hawkins."

"Aye, so. And it provided you with a dowry."

"So my dowry's to be thrown in my face, now?" raged Lady Alice. "Oh, if my husband were still . . . I would not have to endure such . . ." She dabbed her eyes, a flush in her cheeks.

"If you were the man you once were, you'd fit out a ship and go and fetch that bar silver you talk so much of . . ."

The Squire looked alarmed and put his fingers to his lips.

"If my husband were alive, he'd not wait, he'd not sit smoking and gossiping by the fire, he'd . . . Don't you shush me, sir."

The Doctor spoke soothingly. "Lady Alice, that was all fifteen years ago and, as you say, we are all much older . . ."

She shrugged, then recalled why she'd come.

"I insist you send to the kitchen for Betsy and tell her where her duty lies."

The Squire gave me a small nod. Like the old blind horse, that was good enough for me. I slipped out of the room in search of Betsy and Lady Alice never saw me go. I was too quick for someone else, as well. As I pulled open the door, Betsy, who had been bent down outside, leaped back with a swirl of her white dress. I grinned at her.

"I'm to fetch you from the kitchen, Betsy. We'd best mark time ten paces."

So we stepped up and down the passage while I counted to ten, then she went in and shut the door leaving me outside. A lady has her pride. I was tempted to bend down and listen, but I'd no wish to be put on the road again. So I stood back and waited. Moments later, Lady Alice swept out, never once looking at me, and Betsy beckoned me in again. The Squire said:

"Now, Tom. Let's waste no more time. Our lodge keeper shall light you up to Black Hill Cove and take you to Master Hawkins of the Admiral Benbow, who's in need of a boy, being too busy himself with other things these days."

Squire grinned to himself, and Dr Livesey frowned at the indiscretion.

"So, Tom Carter. Betsy shall see you down to the lodge and the lodge keeper will take you the rest of the way. No, don't thank me. Thank the Doctor who picked you up on the road. Just do your work, keep your eyes open and we'll all be well pleased."

Keep my eyes open? Strange thing to say. But it was a strange house altogether I'd stumbled on, with its talk of treasure ships and bar silver and secret ventures. And what was the comely, brown Betsy up to, listening at doors?

All these thoughts, and plenty more, roamed round my head as I set off, along with Betsy, my old canvas jacket over my new shirt, down the drive to the lodge gate.

6

Ben Gunn's Joke

The lodge keeper was a funny old cove, his green livery stained and patched up here and there, and a slight smell of the bottle about him, too. He was wrinkled and brown as a berry with wild grey locks and a habit of dancing round, taking hold of you and talking to himself. I wasn't sure if I should answer him or no, but he didn't seem to mind, but skipped ahead of me with the lantern, like a will-o-the-wisp, and hopping back, chattering all the time.

"Tom Carter is it, eh? and what, says you, is my name? and I tells you, it's Ben Gunn. And you says, a funny old name, for a funny old cove, I'll be bound."

He'd read my thoughts, so he had. Ben Gunn was no fool, even though he couldn't stop jawing.

"A rare, kind man the Squire, says you, and I say, as far as it goes, and it don't go so far these days – a big house and the blackamoors and all. And poor old ignorant Ben Gunn, a Christian and a white man, what has his lodge to keep and is to think himself lucky."

He swung the lamp in my eyes, startling me and drew me by my coat forward along the road, which now wound upwards and got narrower as we climbed. On my right hand I could hear the sea fall on the rocks and draw away over and again, while Ben babbled on.

"I was rich, Tom lad, and says you, 'Never, Ben Gunn, you old sot, rich, never.' But it's true and there's more where that came from. And why don't old Ben go and fetch that bar silver then, if he knows where it is?"

Bar silver again; my ears pricked up.

"Answer is, Tom, to get richer, you have to be rich. Old Squire, if he had the money, he'd be after more. He'd fit out a ship and get over to Treasure Island like a ball from a musket. And for why? asks Tom, and Ben tells him . . ." The lodge keeper held up the lantern so the glass burned my nose and went on:

"So he can get Lady Alice out of the house again, and he and the Doctor can sit in peace round the fire and talk about the old days."

"What?" I cried. "His own daughter?"

"Daughter, says you, and Ben says, never. Lady Alice is Squire's ward. His old friend died and left her for Squire to look after. Aye, and that's all he left. So Squire had to find her one dowry already out of his own pocket. And that didn't come cheap, either. But Squire's a fool."

Ben Gunn looked round: "Not a word of this to a Christian soul, eh, Tom."

I shook my head.

"And why's he a fool? Cause Lady Alice'll marry another husband like the last one and what did he do with her money . . .?"

I waited, my breath still.

"What did he do with her money? Why he did what Ben Gunn did with it, like any gentleman would. And what like is that? asks Tom, and Ben says, why he pissed it up the wall."

"Did he die of drink, then, Ben?"

He did not hear me.

"If you ask me how did he die, I'll tell you, not that you'll believe old Ben. He climbed up on top of Clifton and dived off into the Gorge. He shouted out that he was a seagull and he would shite on all his creditors as they took the waters in the Hotwell down below."

Well well, I thought. Lady Alice's husband wasn't quite

the man she made him out to be, but he was no ordinary mortal.

Ben took my arm. Ahead of us, on the brow of a height, its lights gleaming lonely, was a single building.

"There it is, Tom lad. The Admiral Benbow Inn. 'Tis Jim Hawkins' and 'twas his father's before him. That house has seen rare doings, sea rovers carving each other to carbonado with their cutlasses and cursing dreadful to Christian ears ... that's where Jim got the map ..."

"What map?"

"You ask me, what map, and I says, why the map they would all like to lay their hands on, which tells you the bearings and the lay of the island, with red crosses for the bar silver where it lies under Black Crag."

"And, if he has the map, why doesn't he get off there right away and make himself a rich man?"

I was so quick I got the question in first. Ben Gunn brought up the lantern and I pushed his hand away so he wouldn't singe my eyebrows.

"Because two women keep Jim here. His old mother for one. She nigh lost him when he were your age, fifteen years agone, and she won't let him out of her sight now."

"And the other?"

"Why, Lady Alice, of course, Squire's ward. Our Jim lad worships the ground she treads on."

"Then why won't he make himself rich and wed her?"

"For why – that'd be telling. Tom Carter's going to be Jim Hawkins' boy, ain't he and he can find out a power of things if he keeps his eyes open."

They'd all have me keep my eyes open.

"But if you asks me, then I says, Jim Hawkins is too good for this mortal life and its wickedness. He's a sight too grave for the world."

Benn Gunn suddenly chuckled.

"So you and I, Tom, we play a joke on Jim, eh?"

I wasn't so sure a new lad should start by pulling his master's leg. But Ben wasn't asking my opinion anyway. He handed me the lantern, bent down and picked up a stone from the path by the inn. Then he drew up close to the building and began to tap on a larger stone on the ground – tap tap tap.

As he tapped he sang in a cracked old voice.

> "Fifteen Men on a dead man's chest.
> Yo ho ho and a bottle of rum.
> Drink and the . . ."

I never heard the rest of the verse. A shutter near the inn door was thrown open. There came the flash and crack of a pistol and a ball buzzed like a bee past my ear so close I felt its breath.

I didn't wait for the other barrel. I threw myself down on the ground, dowsing the light as I fell.

7

The Admiral Benbow

As I grovelled in fear on the ground outside the inn door, Ben Gunn who had stayed on his feet in the shadows, now struck up with:

"How sweet the name of Jesu sounds . . ."

in a fine, ringing tenor voice.

The inn door opened abruptly and a woman's voice called.

"'Twas you, Ben Gunn, you villain. Jim said it would be. But I take no chances."

Ben capered up the steps, calling:

"Right you are, Mrs Hawkins. No chances, says you. And no chances says I, which was why I gave the lamp to young Tom here. And likewise no chances says he and dowsed the glim before you could say Cap'n Flint."

"Tom, who's Tom?"

"Why, the new boy that's come to help in the tap and all . . ."

"We don't need a boy," came a man's voice.

"Squire says you do, and says Ben Gunn, Squire's word is law."

"Bring him in. He can stay the night, and we'll set him on the road tomorrow with his breakfast and a shilling."

In we went. It was mid-week and the place had but few folk in it. Less than I might have expected even for a lonely place like this. There was a dreary air to it. Taps should have men in 'em, drinking, arguing the toss, spitting and singing now and then. We passed through a curtain into a parlour at the side. There sat a plump, kindly but severe-looking old lady in a dark dress, with a neat apron over it, some sewing spread out in her lap and a horse pistol laid across that. A youngish broad-shouldered man was closing the shutters. He turned to look at me. He had a fine, though palish face, a brow that showed temper and a thrust out chin. His expression was stern but his eyes were friendly. He looked me over, noting my muddy breeches. He nodded to the bench by the window.

"Sit down, Tom lad.

"Ben, go into the tap and draw yourself a pot – only one, mind you." When Ben was out of earshot, Master Hawkins lowered his voice.

"On the run, eh?"

I nodded.

"You can fool Squire and Doctor, but not me. We have all sorts through here, society men, apprentices and all. I know when they have a ticket and when not. I wish you no harm, Tom, but Mother and I can manage this place without a boy – the custom we get."

"And that's little enough," observed the old lady sharply.

"Mother," answered Master H., "what do we lack?"

"To hear you talk, nothing. The free way you hand our fortune out to all and sundry: journeymen, drovers, beggars and," she wrinkled her nose at the word, "actors."

"Mother – it's little enough each one of them gets, and only in need."

"Aye, you'll give and give till that," she spoke low, "that chest up there's empty."

He laughed. "No need to whisper, Mother. Everyone in the hamlet knows what's up there. And none of 'em, honest or rogue, dares come near it while you sit with your pistol athwart the stairs." Now he lowered his voice again. "What would you have me do? Play the jolly host and drink it away like Ben Gunn, or Lord . . ."

Mrs H. tightened her lips. "And how do you hope to win my fine lady with an empty chest? She'll not look at anyone with less than ten thousand pounds."

That thrust went well home.

"I'll not bandy words over Lady Alice. Mother, do you go to bed. I'll see to things down here. Tom can give me a hand and earn his supper."

Just then someone called in the tap. Might as well show willing, I thought, and went briskly in to serve them.

I drew off a pint from the barrel and sniffed it. The customer eyed me gloomily. I threw it down into the bucket and drew another.

"Won't come any better," grumbled the man, slapping down his halfpenny on the bar.

I bent towards him and whispered, "Is this gnat-piss brewed in the house?"

He shook his head. "Mistress Hawkins is too old now and Lord Jim don't care. He buys it from a brewer ——— way, and they rook him dreadful to behold."

Just then Master Hawkins called from the parlour.

"Have yourself a pot, Tom, lad."

"Thank you kindly, Mr Hawkins, but I supped up at the Hall."

Half an hour later the bar was empty. Even Ben Gunn, seeing there was no more free ale, said goodnight with much winking and nudging and went his way. I pushed back the parlour curtain. Mrs Hawkins had gone upstairs, closing the stair door behind her. But Master Jim sat at the small table, a candle drawn close to him, papers before him, and counting on his fingers. I thought he was making up his reckoning.

But, instead he stared into the distance and muttered:

"Ye fearful cliffs of aspect wild,

"Ye mournful forests of pine and oak."

"Woods, sir," I said.

"Eh, what's that?"

"Woods – would sound better, so would oak and pine."

He did not seem to hear me but went on counting on his fingers. I went back into the tap room, cleared away the pots and washed them. Looking round in the brewhouse at the back I found all the tackle for making ale, and sacks of grain and malt, hard crusted. All was covered in dust. But I found a hammock, too, stowed away in a corner and slung it from a beam. After one or two attempts I heaved myself into it and made ready to sleep. Best get a good night's kip, I thought.

The open road for Tom Carter tomorrow, worse luck. For all their funny ways, I liked Master Jim and his mother, pistol and all. And there was a fine air of mystery about the whole place – Hall, Squire, Doctor, Lady Alice, with the talk of silver, sealed lips, open eyes and what not.

As I drifted off to sleep, I heard him pace the parlour floor, declaiming:

> "Ye fearful cliffs of aspect wild,
> Ye mournful woods of oak and pine."

8

The Playwright

I woke with the dawn, the sound of the waves on the rocks below in my ears. For a moment I could not say where I was, then I remembered. The Admiral Benbow Inn, Black Hill Cove to which I was to bid goodbye with a shilling after breakfast. Heaving myself from the hammock, I went into the kitchen at the side. In a brace of shakes I had a fire going in the range. I rummaged in the larder, found some odds and ends and set some bacon to fry. I found some eggs too and took a fancy to make an omelette in the French style.

By the time the old lady found her way downstairs, I had the table laid in the parlour, platters, mugs and all and the food piping hot. She stared at it but said nothing and set to like a drover on market day. When Master Jim came down I'd to make a second helping and the food was gone – no breakfast for little Tom. So far no word had been spoke, save "Good morrow" and I was at a loss how to prolong the conversation in the hope of getting the Hawkins family to think again about showing me the door.

But right at that moment I was dealt an ace. Outside on the track a brewer's waggon rumbled up. Without giving Master Hawkins a chance to move, not that he showed any signs of that, being too busy tracing words on the table, I nipped outside and caught the drayman as he was about to heave a barrel down.

"None today, thank you," said I.

"What?" he growled, turning to stare at me. He was as broad as a house and with a nasty look to him.

"Master says that last barrel were only fit for sheep dip."

He pushed the barrel back on the cart and took a step towards the inn.

"I'll ask him myself."

"Master's busy. You'll have to talk to Mrs H."

That stopped him. He looked cunning.

"What'll it be then?"

I hopped up on the waggon. Up front under a tarpaulin were more barrels.

"Two of them," I guessed.

"They'm bespoke."

"One then – or . . ."

"Or what?"

"Or – nought."

He made to climb back on the driving seat, but I stopped him with: "Or I tell your master you're watering his brew – more than he does, that is."

A bull's eye. He said no more, but heaved down a couple of barrels of the best and humped them into the tap. I ran in and asked Master Hawkins for the money. The drayman looked at it and said nothing. but he eyed me as though he'd like to wring my neck.

I bid him good day, ran into the tap, tapped the first barrel, tasted it, drew another pot and proudly took it in to Master Jim. He hadn't touched his breakfast. His fine omelette was congealed on his platter. He had shoved it all on one side and was busy with his papers. As I came in he looked up.

"Tom, lad, what do you think? . . .

> 'Oh hear my pledge of vengeance dire,
> My oath, my passioned promise hear.'"

I stood and stared at him. Without thinking I took a deep swig of his ale and said,

"Why not swap oath with pledge, sir?"

He pushed out his lip, shrugged, then began to pace up and down.

> "Oh, hear my oath of vengeance dire,
> My pledge, my passioned promise, hear."

I tiptoed back to the tap, drained my pot, took the broom and began to sweep the floor. When Mrs H. came in later in the morning I was busy measuring out grain and malt. She smiled grimly and went away.

At noon she came back, cut me some bread and meat and talked to me about my family. That took no time at all. When she heard how I was born, she shook her head and went away. That afternoon one or two labourers came in from the fields with jugs. I filled 'em up from the new barrels, gave 'em a free sample pot and watched them go, rubbing my hands.

That night the tap was full, and the next night, and Tom Carter stayed on. If Master Jim remembered saying ought about little Tom going on the road then he said no more about it. All he cared for was the blessed play he was writing called *Prince of the Indies*. Time and again, when I was rushed off my feet in the tap, he would come in, hair wild, paper and pen in his fist and, gripping me by the arm, declaim something like:

"Ruin seize thee, ruthless tyrant."

I'd give him my honest opinion and off he'd go and rework it. It was plain to see he cared not a toss about the custom I'd brought him, the full house, the brewer's man sweet as kiss my hand. But I gave that rogue the order of the boot as soon as our own brew was ready – and sent to Bristol to another house for wines to build up the parlour trade.

Master Jim thought only of his play and the chances of having it put on at the playhouse they'd just opened in

Bristol where the manager was a young chap like himself and where, as you might have guessed, Lady Alice was a regular, as I soon found out from Betsy.

Betsy came down from the Hall once or twice with an order. The Squire saw fit to get his port and Bristol milk through my good offices. She slipped me a shilling which she said would be due me every month, if I "kept my eyes open". I didn't tell her I could make twenty times as much by diddling my master without him being any the wiser. Instead I pocketed the shilling, winked at her and said, "Very good." She had a habit, now and then, of sneaking into the tap where I was busy with my broom.

She'd catch me bending and give my backside a pinch. But if I tried sauce for the goose with her, she'd slip out of the way and glare at me.

But pinches and shillings aside, I kept my eyes open. There were strange things to see and to hear.

And nought was stranger than Master Jim and his play. As it was slowly written, scene by scene he began to bring it at nights into the tap.

Then he would call for glasses all round and force the company to listen to the scene he'd just completed, or even help him read it aloud part by part. In these fits, he was the most over-riding companion ever known and he would slap his hand on the table for silence all round, he would fly up in a passion of anger at a line wrongly uttered or if someone missed his cue, or if he judged the company was not following the action. Nor would he allow anyone to leave until his rehearsal was finished.

Once a farm labourer, greatly daring after a trying evening, burst out with:

"Master Jim. 'Tis all very well for gentlefolks, this, but I'd rather have a good yarn. Do ye read for us your tale about the sea cook."

Master Hawkins rounded on him.

"What tale? There's no such thing."

The lad was abashed but stuck to his guns.

"Why, Master Jim, ye know, those papers you have up in your room, what Squire and Dr Livesey got ye to write down about Treasure Island."

"Aye," chorused the others, "Treasure Island," and one muttered, "and devil take the *Prince of the Indies*."

Master Jim's fury was awful to see. He started towards the luckless lad who backed off in fear. But he thought better and stamped out of the room. We saw him no more in the tap that evening, or for many evenings to come.

That night, though, as I went up to his room with the keys, I found him seated on his bed, a candle by his side, a bundle of papers on his knees and staring into space, his face vacant and boyish looking. I spoke to him. He heard not a word. I left the keys by his side and went to bed.

The following week by chance Dr Livesey was in the parlour. He came partly to see how the old lady did, and partly to sample a new case of Madeira I had up from the port. I put the matter to him. Why was my master so full of passion when the words "Treasure Island" were uttered? Every man talked of his past, soldiers and sailors talked of wars and voyages, why did Master Hawkins guard his past so secretly? To tell truth, it was not only Master Jim I hoped to hear of, but other matters.

But the Doctor looked grim and said, "When Jim was your age he saw men killed like flies. He killed a man himself and was nigh killed in his turn. He wishes to forget and I am not the one to remind him."

I thought – I nearly killed a man. But I said nothing. I had a secret past like my master, and had no desire to rake it up nor have others do it.

But the world is not ruled by one's desire. My next hand at the table, had no ace, but the joker. My past caught up with me.

9

Enter Mr Argent

Autumn and winter passed, without too much excitement. Two years before, bread had been scarce and dear. There were riots, ricks burned and granary doors burst in by hungry folk, troops called in and the hangman was the busiest cove in the county. But two good harvests made that a memory, though a fresh one. Men on the land and in the workshop had coin to spare and I had cause to see this in the tap at the Admiral Benbow. I was busy, so was my master. The inn prospered, which pleased me – and Mrs H. His play was completed which pleased him, and no less the regulars at the Admiral Benbow who could now pass their evenings quietly.

Spring came before we knew where we were. Fresh breezes blew from landward with a tang of green grass and flowers. Then one day the boy rode over from the hamlet with the post, Old Postie being too drunk to manage it. Master Hawkins came into the tap in a high old state. Mistress Hannah More (of whom he was sure I'd heard), one of the patrons of the theatre, and it was said close friends with the famous actor-manager Garrick, had read his play and declared he must go at once to London and see the great man.

He was like a man in a fever for days, not least for thinking how he might persuade his mother to let him out of her sight. But he need not have bothered. The old lady had become somewhat forgetful, not to say short sighted, in the past months. She had slipped back in time and regularly called me Jim, while him she barely noticed. So when he told her with much humming and ha-ing, that he was off to London, she smiled at him, folded her hands over the pistol in her lap and bid him come again and stay longer next time.

He set off next day. The Squire lent him Daniel and the coach to take him all the way into Bristol and get the London flier. Mail coaches never came near our part of the world. Not that I sorrowed over that, despite the loss of trade. I preferred my privacy. Little Tom Carter was liked in the neighbourhood, it seemed, and no questions asked. So I was left in charge, which I was at any rate, so that made no difference. I would sit in the late evenings with the old lady, or drink a glass with the Doctor as he smoked his pipe and very pleasant it was. No one mentioned the past, the present was good enough.

But one morning I heard a coach rattle into the yard and through the window I saw it to be an open carriage with three gentlemen in it, one tall, one small and one broad or fat, you might say. The tall and the short one got out and stretched their legs, the fat one stayed where he was. Perhaps they were passing through, Lord knows where to. I placed a bottle and three glasses on a tray, straightened my apron and stepped out to salute them.

I got no further than the first two paces towards my customers when I was suddenly grabbed from behind and tray, bottle and all went flying.

"What the . . . ?" I cried. My attacker swung me round and I found myself staring right at the two bounty hunters I'd given the slip to last summer. They must have been lying in wait for me by the inn door.

"Little Tommy Carter for sure," they said, grinning all over their ugly mugs. As I struggled with my captors, two men from the coach came closer. The taller one, who spoke with a blunt northern way and a very earnest air, said:

"Come now, sir, let the lad go. What harm has he done th – you?"

"Harm, sir?" said they. "Why, he's a runaway apprentice. He must go back to his master."

"Reason indicates that labour must be free. Such forms of bondage hold the nation's industry in chains," said the tall man deliberately.

"You may be right, sir," said one rogue, "but we know the law."

"Do you now?" said the smaller gentleman, putting in his fourpenn'orth. "I would deny your right to seize this person without proof positive that an offence has been committed. Habeas Corpus, though grievously offended against in recent years, is nevertheless still held sacred in these islands."

The man who had hold of my shirt collar answered: "Habeas Corpus is as maybe, sir. But 'tis we who have the body, and possession is nine tenths of the law – so I've heard."

With that the bounty hunters steered me round my would-be helpers and were leading me past the carriage and towards the road, when the fat man, who had an amiable, broad face, red as a setting sun, spoke up.

"Come nearer, my friends. Let me put to you a proposition."

At the magic word, they wheeled about and came towards the coach, without letting go of me.

"My proposition, friends, is that money overrides both law and custom and even natural justice and is a law and reason unto itself. Do you agree?"

If they did not follow him every inch of the way, they knew where he was driving. They nodded.

"I'll give you five guineas if you let the boy go and leave him be. That's more than you'll get for handing him in, I'll wager."

They looked at one another, then one of them stepped up. The fat man handed him a small purse and he stepped back. Then the other one, who still held me, said: "I take it you mean five guineas each, sir.".

The fat man looked him over amiably, then answered,
"Pray release the boy and step up."

He did so and I smartly placed myself on the other side
of the carriage. Now the bounty hunter stepped close to the
coach, hand held out. Quick as light, the fat man presented
a pistol, an inch from the rogue's nose. His voice, which
had a mellow, almost unctuous tone, suddenly became harder.

"I don't care for your accounting, sir. Now think yourself
fortunate I do not claim back the first five guineas. Up
anchor and away."

At this nautical command, they cast off and ran for it.

Smiling genially, the fat man put away his pistol and began
slowly to get down from the carriage. I stepped forward to
help him, but he waved me off. As he stepped into the yard
he seemed to limp a little but he was brisk enough, as I'd
seen already. He was a striking man, though his face was
broad and plain to be sure. His eyes were deep and sharp.
He had the air of a man of business, a merchant in the sea-
going trade.

I thanked him warmly, but he shook his head.

"Think nothing of it."

"Tom Carter's my name, sir, Mr Hawkins' lad."

A broad smile spread over the fat gentleman's face.

"And how is my very good friend, Mr Hawkins, whom I
have not had the pleasure of cla – of seeing this many a long
year?"

"Well, sir, but not here. He's in London on business."

"Aha, a man of affairs, eh?"

"No, sir, a playwright."

"A playwright. Shiver – bless my soul. Did you hear that
now?" He addressed his friends. "Mr Hawkins a playwright." He turned to me. "My name, Master Carter, is
Argent. Might I call you Tom? Since you are host in Mr
Hawkins' stead, we'll take a glass of that fine sack you had
knocked from your hands by those villains."

"I'm afraid 'tis broke, sir."

"So it is, and I shall pay for that bottle and for another. No, I will do so."

In we went and made ourselves comfortable in the parlour. Mrs Hawkins was abed, feeling a little queer the last day or so, and we had the place to ourselves.

"Now, Tom, this," said Mr Argent, indicating the tall man, "is Mr Somerscale and he is, if you please, a projector, or as some call them these days, an inventor. He plans, believe it or not, to make a carriage run upon rails with the help of steam such as we get from a kettle. Can you credit that now?"

"Reason indicates," said Somerscale, sipping his sack, "that if steam can draw down a rod by making a vacuum, it can also force the rod up by its own power . . ."

"Your reason indicates," interrupted the fat man, "but my economy demands you confine yourself to obliging the steam to work our mine pumps the better."

Having properly squashed Mr Somerscale, Mr Argent turned to the small man.

"This is Mr Wilton, who, as you have observed, is a lawyer, and as such, knows when to hold his peace."

Which Mr Wilton did, contenting himself with drinking his wine and casting his shrewd little eyes about the place. Indeed later when he'd stepped out, so I thought, to find the usual offices, I found him peering around the staircase leading to Master Hawkins' room. He said nothing but thanked me when I steered him towards the rear of the inn.

Well, we spent a pleasant hour together until folk began arriving to be served. Seeing he would get little more talk from me, Mr Argent took his leave, his two assistants following him like hounds on a leash.

Next day he returned, though I'd told him Master Jim would be away several days, and this time he took food with Mrs H. and me, Mr Argent paying for all, and paying handsomely. Altogether I found his company agreeable and the conversation which flowed between him and the Inventor and Lawyer, of deeds, contracts, engines and projects was a source of wonder for me. It was a world beyond that which I knew, of the farm and workshop, a world where money and power of all sorts seemed without limit.

I found the names of his companions confusing at first. But in the end I sorted them out in my mind as Wensleydale and Stilton. The Inventor with his stout body and whey-like face made me think of the one cheese, the Lawyer with his brown, crusty visage, reminded me of the other. These boy's fancies I kept to myself, though.

They came again a third time, in the evening, and stood the house a round. It was a pity, I thought, that neither Dr Livesey nor Ben Gunn were to hand, for they would have found the trio as remarkable as I did.

The strangest thing, though, was that on the day after their final visit, Mr Hawkins came home and when I told him of Mr Argent, my master denied all knowledge of the gentleman. "The name means nothing," he said.

I put that down to the excitement of his trip to London, or should I say, his disappointment. It seems the great Mr Garrick, had told him he had a literary future, but in prose, not blank verse.

That night I heard him rooting around his bedroom as if in search for something. Next day he asked me:

"Tom, I had some papers, a whole bundle. Not my play. Have you seen them?"

"No, Mr Hawkins," said I, which was the truth, in the way he asked the question.

He shook his head. "Well, that's perplexing. I had them underneath my bed. Now they are gone. Strange."

Strange indeed. But just how strange we were soon to learn.

PART

— 2 —

The Sea Lawyer

—— 10 ——

The Map

After mystery, excitement, and none too agreeable. It all started well enough. Betsy came down from the Hall, riding behind Daniel on a great roan, her head held up like a lady, her feet stuck out at the sides like the hoyden she was inclined to be. She brought an invitation to Master Hawkins to take supper with the Squire. There was a note attached, which read "Raisins and wine in the library afterwards," which I took to be some kind of old custom or practical joke between old friends. There was also a note for me, bidding me attend as well and bring a case of port, I'd know which. Indeed I did, one so old and crusted it was marvellous the Squire's leg did not drop right off.

It was a pleasant evening as I observed. For though I took my supper in the kitchen with Betsy, Daniel and the others, I was charged with the choosing and serving of the wine, which meant I was in and out of the dining-hall and after that the library, and if I were to linger a little while they talked no one seemed to notice. Those who are waited on do not pay heed to those who wait, unless of course, their plate or cup is empty.

Once, as I came from the cellar with the brandy, I spied Betsy at her listening post by the library door. I took the chance to pinch her rump rounded so invitingly as she bent over. She swivelled round, seized my wrist in an iron grip, brought her chestnut-brown cheeks and snub nose close to mine and said:

"Breathe a word and I'll bite your nose off." She made a

55

pass at me with her white teeth, then swung away down the passage.

Inside the library I found the Squire and Doctor smoking over the fireplace in consideration, I supposed, for Lady Alice who sat at the end of the settee on the other side of the room, looking elegant and bored in black and white lace, while at the other end sat Master Jim, looking pale, stern and handsome and doing his best to converse across six feet of empty air.

By his side was a plate full of raisins which he chewed between sips of wine. A strange mixture I thought, for I prefer cheese with my wines if anything, but then no accounting for taste as the man said when he saw the Frenchman eat frogs' legs.

There was a tense air about the four of them. I'd entered in the middle of a dispute. The temptation was too great. I served the brandy, then walked to the door, opened it and closed it again, while staying on the inside, in the shadows outside fire and candle light. My deception was rewarded, as deception sometimes is, else why would folk practise it?

The Squire, knocking out his pipe, began to speak.

"Jim, lad, look at it this way. The signs are right. You know our family has had its share of bad luck of late." Master Jim looked with sympathy towards Lady Alice, but she ignored him. "For better or worse," Squire went on, "our fortune's drained away. We've been hard put to maintain this Hall as it should be, and Lady Alice . . ."

"Do be about the business, sir," his ward interrupted him.

"But now, Jim, lad, Fate seems to smile on us. There are signs. First, Blandly the agent down in Bristol – you remember him? – sends me a jewel of a servant, Betsy. What's more, she's bought for a song at a time when you could not buy her like for fifty golden guineas.

"Then, on top of that, this splendid fellow sends me word

that he knows of a venture I can have a share in, eighth or quarter, according to means. Copperware to Benin, blackamoors to Kingston and sugar to Bristol. Safe as the Mint he reckons and nearly as rich."

Master Jim looked puzzled.

"I'd be glad to help you with what I have, Mr Trelawney, as you well know, but that's not near enough to buy shares of that kind."

Lady Alice looked her contempt at my master.

"Fiddlesticks, Jim, lad," said the Squire. "Do pay heed."

The Doctor looked into the fire with a queer, embarrassed expression on his face.

"First," went on Squire, "I need to get into the Merchant Venturers' Company. Well that's not so hard as it sounds. Blandly knows a gentleman or two, good King and Country men, none of your damned Whigs or Quakers, who'd be glad to have me in the Venturers' to strengthen their hand and bring a touch of weight to the debates."

The Doctor's pipe snapped. The Squire glared at him.

"That being so, all I need is capital, Jim lad."

"That I see, Mr Trelawney, sir. How will you raise it?"

"Raise is the word, Jim," answered the Squire, shifting his leg in agitation, then wincing with pain. "Why – the bar silver. The bar silver. With two thousand I can raise an expedition. If my guess is right, there may be a quarter of a million in that cache, the market being what it is. Enough to launch a fleet to the Indies, enough to roll in, to play duck and drake with . . ."

The Doctor raised his head: "Trelawney, old friend, caution. Those words were used before and prophetic they proved."

"Hmph," muttered the Squire, sucking at his port. "What do you say, Jim, to another voyage, if I can scrape the money together? Blandly will find us a ship . . ."

"By your leave, you trust that rogue too much," interrupted

the Doctor, but Squire paid him no heed and ran on:

"Come, Jim, what do you say? A partnership. The four of us in this room (I shrank further into the shadows). We'll divide four ways, none of this owner-captain-officer-crew share business this time."

Jim rose from the couch, his face paler than before. Whether those raisins lay heavy on his stomach or whether he was otherwise upset, wasn't clear at first. His voice was calm.

"No, sir, I would not agree," he said.

Squire burst out: "I know what you said, damme – oxen and wain ropes wouldn't drag you back. Nonsense, a glorious venture it was and the right triumphed in the end, as it will again. Come, Jim."

"No, sir." How Master Jim could fail to see the look Lady Alice was giving him along the settee, I cannot think. She was torn between pride and something else – a wish to plead with him. In the end, pride won. She kept her mouth shut.

"Then, Jim, I'll thank you to let me have the map back. You know we need it for the bearings, the soundings, and all. You are the only one who knows latitude and longitude, hang it."

"That map, Mr Trelawney, was given into my safe keeping, to prevent others from sailing to that island and repeating that sorry tale, not for you to begin again, at your age. I must ask you to excuse me, sir."

With that he bowed to Lady Alice, nodded to the Doctor and marched out, Tom Carter nipping out smartly before him. Behind us I heard a crash as the Squire hurled his glass into the fireplace.

—— II ——

We Go to Bristol

No coach home for us that night. We walked on the cliff path, Tom Carter going before with a lantern, Master Hawkins following after in silence. As we reached the Admiral Benbow and crept inside, taking care not to waken the old lady with her hasty trigger finger, my master turned to me at last.

"Well, Tom, Squire Trelawney thinks I'm a fool. Lady Alice thinks I'm a coward. What do you think? Come now, Tom, I know you heard every word that passed. Speak truth."

Folk rarely mean that when they say it. However, in for a penny, in for a pound.

"The one's true, t'other isn't. It takes a man to stand up as you did tonight, Master Hawkins. Squire thinks you're a fool because he wants his hands on that bar silver." I hesitated an instant, then pushed on.

"For the same reason, I think you're a fool, too. Lady Alice knows you're not a coward, but she's no different from Squire, all she's after is the money to get herself a new husband," I couldn't stop myself, "then she'll not look at you."

That did it. "Hold your tongue, Tom," he shouted.

"Who's there?" called the old lady down the stairs, in the nick of time before Master Jim knocked me half across the tap room. Instead he stamped out.

So, we had sulks for a week. Master Jim sulked around the Inn and wouldn't talk to me. Squire Trelawney sulked up at the Hall. I didn't take it too hard though. My master was sulking out of love, poor soul. The Squire was sulking out of greed. And neither the Doctor nor I, as we admitted to each other over a glass of Bristol milk one night, could find the medicine to cure 'em.

"Time cures all, Tom, lad," said the Doctor, putting his pipe back in the rack I kept for good customers over the fireplace and setting his wig straight.

It didn't do too badly. After a week had gone by, Squire was in high spirits again. Down came Betsy with a message.

He was to be admitted to the Merchant Venturers' in Bristol in two days' time and we were to go with him and share in his honour. His town house in Clifton, hard by the Hotwell, empty for a couple of seasons, had been opened up and I was to go along as well, bringing a dozen of claret for His Nibs. I could ride on the top with Daniel and Betsy (couldn't I just). Mrs H. was happy to see to the inn, only warning me (thinking I was young Jim) to watch out for those greedy-eyed Bristol jades. I'd no notion how the old lady might know what went on in the big city, but she was positive it was a sink of iniquity. I looked forward to it all the more.

My old fears of going into towns to the east had been blown away when my new benefactor, Mr Argent, had given the bounty hunters the order of the boot. Thinking about him reminded me he'd not been seen at the Admiral Benbow since. For all his keenness to see Master Jim, he'd not shown his face there. Still, men of substance are a law unto themselves, as I knew very well.

We were off at crack of dawn next day; Squire, Doctor, Lady Alice and Master Jim inside; Daniel, Betsy and me on top, me on the outside with my arm round Betsy's waist to steady her. She did the same for me, and every now and then would give me a little hug that nearly cracked my ribs. A day's ride and we came into the city over the new bridge, chock-a-block with waggons and carriages. It beat me why they were all so proud of it, but they reckoned the old one was worse. There's progress for you. Then, on to the house at the Hotwell, which is tucked away over the river and under the great cliffs that rise up to Clifton Down. They say that in spring and summer that's a fine scented place for lads and lasses to go walking, but I never found out if that were true. We'd more than enough to do.

At supper that night, Squire was in grand form. In fact he seemed to be doing his best to coax Master Jim back into a good humour. A funny old buffer, Mr Trelawney, but no harm in him, I thought. I changed my mind later, but never mind.

Lady Alice gave nothing for nothing. She hardly had two civil words to put together for my master. Even next day when we all set out for Merchants' Hall and Master Jim, looking very fine, so I thought, in a dark-blue tailed coat, walked beside her sedan chair, chatting about the weather and the scene, she was condescending and no more.

It was a fine day and as we walked along we got the full flavour of the city, the ships all jammed together in the river, their masts leaning this way and that as the tide left them high and dry. They reckoned this was the second richest port in England but they grudged every penny they might spend on a new dock. So long as the cargoes got in and out, what did they care? There were the quality in their silks and brocades, buzzing around the Hotwell like flies round a lump of meat, and the merchants in their sober dress, the skippers casting their eye at the sky and all around them servants and porters, sailors in town off the ships. We'd to push every inch of the way. The sun was well up and we got the full flavour of the city, as I said, from the rubbish in the runnels. But nobody seemed to give a hang. They shoved and pushed and argued and shouted and nodded and bowed, as though they were God's gift to the world.

Half the crowd, it seemed, was bound for the same place as we, and at last we were all swept up under the pillars outside the Hall entrance. Once inside, the Squire, looking very grand for all his hobbling on a stick, looks about him, nodding to this gent and scowling at that. Men, who stood in groups of two or three gossiping, eyed us, nudged each other and winked or turned their backs. There was a strange air about some of them as though they were waiting for something to happen and weren't sure if it would turn out well or badly.

"Mr Trelawney, sir."

"Ah, Blandly."

"At your service, sir, Lady Alice, Dr Livesey, Mr Hawkins . . ."

He was a smarmy creature, this one who came up now.

He was small and plump with eyes that seemed to be all over the place. The Doctor didn't care for him, I'd wager, but the Squire seemed to like him well enough.

"I thought the Company Master might have been out to greet us, Blandly," said the Squire casting his eye round the crowd in the ante-room.

"He'll be here, by and by, sir," said Blandly, giving his hands a dry wash as he talked. He shot a quick look behind him then came closer.

"You understand, sir, a company like the Merchant Venturers' has all sorts, it takes such to make a world, don't you know. There are currents and crosswinds, the folk outside know nought of."

The Squire took that very ill. "Are you saying it ain't cut and dried, Blandly? You gave me to understand it would go through on the nod."

A score of gentlemen must have turned round at that for the Squire's whisper would carry against a gale. Blandly looked sick and put his finger to his lips.

"You understand, sir. There are all sorts . . ."

"You said that before, damme."

". . . There are Church and country men, who are glad to

see such as yourself, sir and then there are the Whigs and Dissenters who aren't so warm, then there are those in the slave trade and there are the Quakers who've cooled off it somewhat of late. There are those who are for the Americans and the America trade and those who think King George is right to give 'em a touch of the whip, there are free traders and tariff men. They fall out at the drop of a hat and . . ."

"You mean we'll be objected to?" The Squire's face began to purple up and the Doctor took his arm as if to feel his pulse.

"Here's the Master now," said Blandly, much relieved.

The Master, portly in a green coat and just as stately as Trelawney, gave him the nod in a friendly manner, though he looked ill at ease.

"What's this, Master?" growled Trelawney.

But the Master was no Blandly. He stared the Squire down ever so courteously.

"Good day, Mr Trelawney, sir. Honoured to have you with us. Have to tell you, however, sir, that a most unusual circumstance has arisen, not of our wishing."

"What's that, sir?"

"An objection, sir."

"To me?" You'd have thought high treason was on the cards.

"A respected member of our company, a proxy member I should say, prominent in Kingston society, has asked that certain matters be placed before our full company, to assist us in considering your acceptance."

"What matters?"

"That is not within my knowledge. All I have been told is that the member will be present today, having lately come from Jamaica."

"What member?"

"Mr Argent, sir." My ears pricked up at that. This promised to be exciting.

"Never heard of him."

The master looked shocked. "Then, sir, you must be the one person with pretensions to the West India trade who has not."

Trelawney looked at Dr Livesey, who looked puzzled. Then he turned to his ward.

"Not some partner of your late husband, m'dear?"

Lady Alice shook her head, disdainful and intrigued at one and the same time. The Master hurried on.

"So, Mr Trelawney, sir, we have departed a little from our normal way of proceeding. We shall foregather without formality in the inner hall, to hear Mr Argent, and to hear what you may have to say. Happily all will be speedily resolved and then we may proceed to accept you. To ensure that there shall be no partiality, we have asked the Recorder of Bristol to be with us today and to take my place. You, of course, may be accompanied by all your party."

"The Recorder," said Trelawney. "That Whig scoundrel?"

At these words, a small gentleman not a dozen paces from us, a man with an extremely ugly face and sharp eyes turned and bowed amiably to the Squire.

The Master signalled to the Company Beadle who stood by the inner door. He rapped on the floor with his staff and in we all went, several score all told. After some shuffling everyone had their place in a great double semi-circle of seats, the Recorder perched on a gilded chair on a dais in front of us. He looked at the Company Master, who turned to the Clerk.

"Where's Mr Argent?"

"Coming, sir, right away."

The double doors at the further end of the Hall, swung open. I spotted Mr Argent first, broad, genial, magnificently dressed, limping a little as he walked. On his right was old Wensleydale, tall and pale, and on his left old Wilton-Stilton, crabbed, small and dark.

As he entered, the company rose. So did the Squire, Dr Livesey and Master Jim. Or, to be more precise, they bounded out of their places as if shot from a gun.

"By heaven!" said the Squire. "Long John Silver on two legs."

Mr Argent bowed.

"At your service, Mr Trelawney."

— 12 —

Mr Argent's Surprise

The company sat down, Dr Livesey and Master Jim using a little force to lower the Squire into his seat from where he glared at Mr Argent with an expression so full of hate that he ought to have been struck dead on the spot.

On the contrary however, that gentleman beamed back at our party with such warmth that for a moment I thought Squire and he had got each other mixed up with two other persons.

"That unmitigated rogue, has the limitless audacity, the effrontery, to . . ."

"Hush," whispered several merchants behind us, and one said distinctly, "Trelawney thinks he's on the bench. But he ain't, he's in the dock."

There were chuckles at that and I thought the Squire would fly apart in his rage. But Mr Argent was addressing the Recorder.

"By your leave and that of this auspicious company, sir, I will sit down. As some of you know, an old wound in the country's service . . ."

"Fiddlesticks," burst out the Squire, and the Doctor smiled.

"Severed my leg," went on Mr Argent. "Thanks to the remarkable inventive powers of Mr Somerscale, I am equipped with a false limb, but I find that to be on my feet – mine and his, that is – is fatiguing. Mr Wilton, who as you know is a respected member of the Bar, will speak for me."

Mr Wilton was on his feet in an instant, bowing right and

66

left and speaking slowly and clearly in that rusty voice of his.

"The matter, sir, concerns a voyage made by Mr Argent, some fifteen years ago, as cook in the employ of Mr Trelawney, who also sailed on the voyage, on the vessel, *Hispaniola*, a schooner of three hundred tons, bound for an island to the west. The promoters of the voyage, then and since, kept its location a close secret. But among those individuals known as 'gentlemen of fortune' it was called 'Treasure Island'."

At these words there was a stir among the merchants.

"Fifteen years, sir, is a long time. Men's memories grow dim. But we are fortunate in that a document has come into our hands, written soon after that voyage by one James Hawkins, cabin boy on the *Hispaniola*."

Master Jim was on his feet, but the Recorder courteously bid him sit down and he obeyed.

"Some may say we should treat this document lightly, as youthful fancies. But on the contrary, sir, we may judge from the first sentence written here, that the whole was written down at the request of the owner of the *Hispaniola*, and his physician and confederate Dr Livesey."

The Doctor grinned at this. Nothing could get his goat.

"I will try to summarize briefly the events of that voyage. We, sir, are accustomed to the hazards of the sea, but I will tell you that of the ship's company of twenty-six, only six came home to Bristol, four of whom, sir, are in this room."

Heads turned at this, but Wilton went on.

"Most of the crew died, not from the elements, nor even of 'drink and the devil' as the old sea song has it, but at the hands of Trelawney and his group. And even the cabin boy, Hawkins, at fourteen was not too young for slaughter, shooting down the coxswain of the vessel."

A cry of outrage came from Master Hawkins, but Wilton continued: "I do not invent these things. They are recorded in the handwriting of Mr Hawkins."

The Recorder bent forward. "I suspect that we shall hear more that is disagreeable. But pray remember this is not a court of law but an inquiry. Mr Trelawney and the others will have their chance to speak, and even to say what they deem needful about Mr Argent."

The Squire upped at that.

"I can say all that's needful in a word. The man's a murdering pirate."

Amid the uproar, Wilton, pitching his voice higher, cried:

"Pirate, sir, what is that word? Did not good Queen Bess call the gallant Sir Francis Drake 'my deare pyrat'? Have not citizens of this port, including some in this very room, had the name 'pirate' hurled at them by some foreign merchant who had good cause to complain of their courage and audacity? And is not our city the richer and prouder for them?"

Now the merchants and skippers were on their feet, cheering. Wilton waved them down and spoke further: "Pirates, sir, are those who kill to secure treasure that is not theirs by right. By that token, sir, what shall we call Mr Trelawney and his friends?

"'Hang the treasure,' said Mr Trelawney, so we are told, 'it's the glory of the sea.' But on another occasion he said 'money to roll in, to play duck and drake with for ever', and by all accounts, sir, that is what he did."

The company roared with laughter.

The Recorder put a frown on his face and said: "Mr Wilton. Confine your remarks to the matter in hand: the voyage."

"Voyage, sir? It was a trail of blood from start to finish. Beginning when young Hawkins and his mother took from a dead sailor's chest a map showing where lay £700,000 in gold, the plunder of one Captain Flint. The theft of the map swiftly brought on the death of a man, a," Wilton paused, "a blind man, sir. You may well be shocked, gentlemen, but I can shock you more. Mr Trelawney, how did he greet this incident? I will tell you. He said: 'An act of virtue, like stamping on a cockroach.' We are clearly dealing with no ordinary country squire, but a man of some calibre, a West Country Ghengis Khan."

"Mr Wilton," said the Recorder. "Let us have the account unembroidered."

Mr Wilton bowed.

"The young boy did what you would think was a just and intelligent thing. Indeed I may say here that my client has the warmest regard for the young man whose qualities have, despite the company he kept, remained almost unsullied."

I saw Mr Argent beam broadly at Master Jim, who turned his head away . . .

"Mr Hawkins gave the map into the safe keeping of a local magistrate. Admirable, but unwise. That magistrate, together with Squire Trelawney, planned, I might say plotted, to seize that treasure for his own private gain. To cut the account short, they hired a crew – with the indispensable help of my client, who, though only a cook, was a man of talents."

"Indeed he was," growled the Squire.

"But this crew, they did not propose to trust. From the beginning they behaved as though they expected mutiny, though as the ship's master Tobias Smollett said, no captain should sail if he suspected such."

At which all the skippers in the Hall nodded wisely.

"They moved the arms and powder, making a fortress around the captain's cabin, and later armed the Squire's personal servants. They created a private army, sir, something outside the law in this realm, since the days of Henry VII.

"Arrived at the island, they sent two-thirds of the crew

ashore on a pretext. The crew were restless, with good reason. My client, however, did his best, as Hawkins testifies, to keep them in good humour. While most of the crew were ashore, Trelawney and his party threatened the other sailors with death if they signalled their shipmates. They then ferried arms and powder secretly to the shore and made a second stronghold in an old pirate stockade. To secure it, they fired, unprovoked, on several of the crew, killing one of them.

"The account shows that during that unhappy voyage, Mr Argent and the majority of the crew fired only when fired upon."

"He stabbed a man in the back," cried Master Hawkins.

"So you say, Mr Hawkins. Your account also shows that one of your party murdered one of Mr Argent's friends in his sleep."

"Ben Gunn did that," cried Master Jim.

"Ah, so it was Ben Gunn, was it? Well, we shall hear more of that gentleman in a moment," answered Wilton calmly.

"What we had in this case, sirs, was a very strange thing, a plot by the ship's owner and master against their crew, a mutiny in reverse. And on what evidence? A conversation overheard by a boy in an apple barrel.

"My client, despite provocation, remained willing to talk under flag of truce. After the cabin boy had shot down the coxswain and set the ship adrift, and the crew were ready, with somewhat understandable fury, to kill him, Mr Argent intervened to save his life, not once, but more than once.

"Only when virtually alone, with the death of other crew members, and discovering that Trelawney and his party had the upper hand, did my client feel he must submit."

"Aye," called the Squire, "and if he hadn't stolen three hundred guineas and run away, his neck might have been longer today."

Mr Argent nodded amiably, and Mr Wilton raised his eyebrows.

"My client was promised, if you please, that they would not prosecute. You may well smile, gentlemen. How would you yourselves value such a promise from men who had disposed of twenty of a company of twenty-six? Well, he took three hundred guineas. The aforesaid Ben Gunn, who helped Trelawney's party against his own former shipmates, was given one thousand pounds for his pains. One thousand out of seven hundred thousand.

"If this, sir, had been a privateer or even a pirate ship, Ben Gunn would have been entitled not to one thousand pounds, but somewhat more. Trelawney, as owner, might have had half the value of the prize, the captain five or six shares, the officers between three and one and a half, according to rank, and the crew members one share each. At the most modest estimate, Ben Gunn should have received nearly fifty thousand pounds.

"No wonder this 'prize' was not submitted to the arbitration of the Admiralty Prize Court.

"But shall we say, this was not a prize, it was buried treasure. Within the King's domain, that is treasure trove. But then perhaps Trelawney considered the island to lie outside the King's domains."

"Rubbish," boomed the Squire. "We hoisted the Union Jack as soon as we landed."

"Then, sir, we shall ask, does the Crown know of this island? I think not. No one save Mr Trelawney's party even knows its latitude or longitude. Had the Crown been informed of this treasure, we may well expect it to have taken its legitimate share. Have we not here an act not only of greed, but of disloyalty, treason almost?"

Suddenly the company was in a fine to do, the Squire's friends and their rivals shouting each other down. In a quiet moment, one bearded skipper pointed at Trelawney and yelled:

"King and Country man, are you, eh? Which King? Which country? I'll wager you're a damned Rechabite. A Jebusite. No, hang it, a confounded Jacobite, a rebel against the Crown."

"I'll have your hide for that," bellowed the Squire. "Damned Whig. I'll lay your grandfather fought for Monmouth the traitor."

"And what if he did?"

"And his father helped murder King Charles The First!" The Squire was well in his stride now.

"Caballero!"

"Roundhead!"

"Puritan!"

"Papist!"

Thump, thump, thump, went the Beadle's stick. The Recorder was on his feet, his face grim, his eyes twinkling.

"Order, order, order. We must not have such tumult. Come, gentlemen, it is time to break our fast. To allow our tempers to cool, I propose we adjourn at least until tomorrow."

"Sir," Mr Argent lumbered to his feet. "I have an even better plan. This afternoon at two of the clock, at the Three Feathers, towards Kingswood Down, there is to be a pugilistic bout. Jem Morris and the lady bruiser Molly Brindle are to challenge all comers. I would bid everyone be my guest at table at noon. We shall eat alfresco outside the Three Feathers. All of you, and in particular old shipmates from the *Hispaniola*, are welcome, to show that though we seek the truth, we do not do so out of malice. Gentlemen, your servant."

With a shout of, "Ho for the Three Feathers," the Recorder, Master and the company headed for the door. Dignity went by the board for the sake of speed. In a moment we were left alone.

"He can go to the Devil," cried the Squire.

The Doctor wagged his head.

"No sir. We must accept his invitation. We must watch him like hawks. Long John, or Argent as he calls himself, is up to something. There's more in this than meets the eye."

—— 13 ——

The Boxing Match

Soon after noon that day, the Squire's coach, with Daniel at the reins, Betsy and me at his side and the rest of the party stowed inside, rolled through the Lawford Gate (where the old gate once stood at any rate) and headed east towards Kingswood. Ahead of us and to our rear stretched out a winding column of coaches, chaises, phaetons, vehicles open and closed, sedans carried by sweating chairmen, ladies and gents on horseback, all half-seen through the dust they kicked up.

The sky was darker here, though the sun shone, for over the dust there hung a heavier cloud that swelled up from a score of pointed buildings, where they made the famous Bristol glass, so I was told. Around the glasshouses, foundries and workshops and tanneries gave out their fumes and soot. But soon enough we were out of the haze and into open ground and a desolate place it was, with gaping holes dug in the hollows and gullies that cut down south to the river. Here and there were great engine pumps with cross beams that rose and fell like giant nodding horses' heads. If the smoke turned my guts, this mournful clanking and chugging filled my heart with gloom. Time and again on evenings in the Admiral Benbow I'd heard old Wensleydale talk of great powers that would make us all rich, a paradise for all. But if that were so, then the road to it must lie through hell, thought I.

Now we left it all behind and were in a stretch of heath, where the carriages and horses turned aside into the yard of an inn so long and high you could have lost the Benbow inside it. And in front, with servants round it like bees round the hive was a long table all draped in white cloth. There must have been a hundred places at least, all laid with shining cutlery and white china. As we rolled in, the table was filling up and at the head, of course, sat Mr Argent, face aglow with good spirits, calling out his orders, waving and beckoning, directing his guests here and there. But the seats around him were kept free.

No sooner had he seen us when he was on his feet, limping over to the carriage.

"Ah, my special guests. This way, Mr Trelawney, sir, madame," he gave his arm to Lady Alice, "Dr Livesey, sir, and, shiv – bless my soul, Jim, lad, no, I beg your pardon, Mr Hawkins, your servant, sir. Why, it's like yesterday, makes me feel young again, though," and he turned and grimaced at Lady Alice, "I shan't see sixty again."

I was dumbstruck, and I reckoned so was Master Jim to see how she dropped her cool expression and acted like a girl at her first ball, letting him lead her away to a place on his right. I noticed something else, too. Her black dress had gone, she was in pale blue and very handsome too. Ho, ho, I thought, off with the mourning and on to the prize fight. With just as much ceremony he had Master Jim placed on the other side of Lady Alice and snapped his fingers to a servant, saying, "See Mr Hawkins has raisins on his side plate, and the best Madeira." Master Jim was silent and I could see Mr Argent would have a hard task putting him in good humour. But was he put off? Not a bit. In between seeing Mr Trelawney and the Doctor to their seats he joked with him.

"You'll wonder how Cap'n Flint does, eh, Jim? I may still call you Jim? Well the old parrot still lives, credit it or not, three hundred years old, if she's a day. But not as spry as before and inclined to stay at home. Her master, though, likes to get about, so he does."

With a manner that was impudent, if not downright effrontery, he turned to Lady Alice, slipping down his white stocking to show her his false leg. "'Tis counterfeit, see the joints and bolts, is it not remarkable? But the rest is as God made it," he chuckled making a nudging movement with his elbow. She put on a show of blushing and flicked his hand with her handkerchief. I did not know where to hide my grin, but a sight of Master Jim's white face quite put me off the joke.

Now I was busy enough, helping Daniel put the horses to grass, and serving the wine.

Would you believe it? Squire had brought up with him the dozen of claret I'd sent up from the Admiral Benbow. With a very civil air, he presented these at table, and without a blush, Mr Argent accepted them. Ten minutes later they were complimenting and toasting each other. If I had not seen what happened in the Merchants' Hall that very morning, I would never have known they'd been sworn enemies. Still, as I've noted before, men of substance are a law unto themselves. Or could Squire be up to something himself?

There was more that caught my attention. In the middle of the feasting, as I went to and fro with the bottles, I passed the head of the table and saw that Mr Argent was not in his place. Nought strange in that since a man must go about his lawful occasions when he dines. But as I returned to the carriage for a fresh supply of wine, I caught in the corner of my eye a quick flick of white. Over on my left was Betsy half concealed at the corner of the inn verandah. She was talking to someone – in earnest too – not joking with a fellow servant. She moved aside then and I saw that beyond her stood none other than Mr Argent. Now that was strange.

No, by the mark, not strange at all. All was clear. Betsy's spying and questioning, how Mr Argent seemed to know all that was afoot. He'd had his eye on us all, through her, for months now. Who knows, he might have slipped her into the Squire's service. But did that mean Blandly was in with him? – a slippery customer that one. There was more to be found out by keeping my eyes open. Time to earn my monthly shilling I thought, whoever was paying it.

By now one hundred sets of cutlery were making a great din in the summer air under the trees by the inn. I stepped aside to have a bite to eat myself. Beyond the noise of the guests at table I could hear another sound, vaster and deeper, like the sea on the rocks at Black Hill Cove. I looked past the screen of bushes round the inn garden and was struck with amazement.

Some four score yards away was a dip in the ground, like a dell, bowl-shaped and shallow. In the centre of it ropes marked off a space of turf. Around this the great bowl was full of folk grown like daisies out of the soil. Daisies they were not though, but a rough lot, men in brass-buttoned jackets and long breeches, women in gaudy dresses and jaunty ribboned bonnets. As I watched them, a small group of men left the crowd, climbed the slope and came towards me as I stood, apron round my waist and cloth over my arm. The leader was a man taller than I'd ever seen before, a good six foot six, lean as a whippet and with a face both sad and humorous at the same time. He spoke to me as they came up.

"Say, lad, do you know Mr Argent?"

I nodded.

"Oblige us will you then, by telling him that Ned Barker and a deputation from the Kingswood colliers want a word with him before the match."

I went back to the table and found the company at their tobacco. Mr Argent had a long cheroot between his lips. He glanced up sharply as I whispered in his ear and stared at the party which halted, caps to their chests, a few yards away.

"Come aboard, Mr Barker," he said.

"We take the liberty, Mr Argent, of speaking to you as chief shareholder, not having satisfaction from your agent."

"What's this?" Argent was bluff, but not so gracious now.

"Mr Argent. You're set on putting the engine in at more pits?"

"I am. The engine pumps out the water, you gentlemen go deeper in, out comes more coal, and more coin goes into my pockets and yours." He turned to Squire as if to get his approval. Mr Trelawney nodded gravely. The Doctor's eyebrows rose a little.

Said Ned Barker, "There's one matter you overlooked, Mr Argent."

"What's that?"

"Lives, Mr Argent. The deeper in we get, the more men are in danger. If your engines fail, and fail they do, men lose their lives. You cannot run for it two hundred feet below as you can in the drifts."

"Barker," answered Mr Argent, looking him in the eye and puffing out smoke, "I never heard a sailor say, 'I won't go to sea, I might get drowned.'"

The company within earshot chuckled, and Ned Barker's lips rose a bit, too.

"Aye, but the crew would be right to refuse to sail in a leaky ship," said he.

"What might that mean?"

"Why this, Mr Argent. We shall work where the engine is put in, if the price is right. If not, then your engine may pump till it bursts, it will not pump up coal by itself."

"Is that a threat, Mr Barker?"

"That's a promise, Mr Argent."

"Then you can go to the Devil with your promise."

"Hear, hear," said the Squire. Jim Hawkins frowned a little at this. Barker answered with a little lift of the eyebrows.

"I warned you, Mr Argent, and it's fair I should. This ship of yours is headed for the rocks. Look out for squalls."

With that, the colliers turned about and went back towards the crowd, leaving Mr Argent and the Squire looking at one another.

Right then a great shout went up.

"Who's our lad? Jem Morris is our lad."

The match was ready to start. Mr Argent said: "What shall it be, Mr Trelawney, one hundred guineas on Jem?"

Squire grinned. "Wait and see," he said.

Fall of the Champion

The gentry – to a gent, and a lady, left the tables and hurried to the match. A space had been cleared for them and the crowd made way in good humour, though not without some remarks on their dress and appearance. But these died away as a man in a bright green jacket climbed through the ropes at the centre and held up his arms.

"My lords, ladies and gentlemen. The colliers' champion, who challenges all comers to ten rounds, ten rounds only, good sirs, for he don't anticipate any one to last longer. My lords, ladies and gents, Jem Morris."

Cheer after cheer went up as Jem Morris slipped into the ring. What a bruiser was Jem. I'd never seen his like, built like a bull, head shaven grey, his massive back scarred as though he'd been beaten with iron rods. He stood in the middle a moment, then moved slowly and heavily from one corner to another, meeting the cheers of his supporters with a kingly wave of his hand. Supporters? I thought as I wriggled through the throng to get as close to the slaughter as I might. Is there anyone here that dares oppose him?

I spoke truer than I knew. Suddenly the babel of chatter and calling around me from that great sweaty multitude under the hot sun, changed note, as the band does when the leader waves his stick. It chilled my blood to hear it, a mixture of insults, shouts of rage, cat-calls and whistles.

Inside the ropes, Green-jacket was saying that the challenger who had come up from Gloucester to fight Jem had withdrawn at the last moment.

"He is even now on his way to Bristol," added Green-jacket by way of embroidery, "from where he proposes to take ship this very night, for Virginia."

He got a laugh for that one but the crowd was ill-pleased, the cat-calls and jeering went on, and as I struggled through to the middle I could see Green-jacket looked sick.

At the moment they were jeering the challenger whose nerve had failed and whose guts had turned to water. Who could blame him? Jem, with his ugly damaged mug and his chest like a stone wall overgrown with grey moss, was enough to take the heart out of any challenger. What would happen now if another man was not found?

"All comers," shouted Green-jacket, hoarse and squeaking somewhat. "Jem intimates to me that he will fight any two men five rounds together, or any man ten rounds one hand behind his back. He'll fight . . ."

A clod of grass flying from the crowd caught him in mid-sentence. After it came a dozen more. Some of the missiles flew over his head and showered the gentlefolk on the far side. They landed around Mr A. and his party where they sat in splendour. Could that be by chance? I began to make my way around the inner circle of the crowd to get closer to my friends. I didn't want to be alone if the crowd started looking for scapegoats. I had got half way round, when in the midst of the clod-shower, over the ropes soared something black and three-cornered, dropping like a crow to land at Green-jacket's feet. He held up the hat for all to see and the clods stopped falling as though by magic.

"A challenger," he bawled. "Who is this bold man? Where does he come from? Which Bedlam has released him for the day?"

From one corner of the circle came a figure who vaulted over the ropes to tower over Green-jacket. Tall and broad, his black muscles a-ripple over his blue coachman's breeches, it was Daniel.

"Who are you, sir?" demanded Green-jacket. He shook his head at the answer.

"Our challenger don't have the King's English."

Someone on the gentry side shouted, "It's Daniel. Squire Trelawney's man."

From the crowd: "He's a slave. Jem don't fight with slaves. That's no match." There were cheers and counter cheers at that.

Jem settled the matter by raising his fist. "I'll fight him whoever he is. As for the King's English, we ain't a-going to talk are we, mate?" and with that he held out his great paw and rapped Daniel on the knuckles.

Almost before Green-jacket had time to get clear of the ring and the seconds to drop their dice and cards and come to the corners, they'd squared up and laid into each other, like stags locking horns in the rutting season.

Jem landed the first blow on Daniel's arm. He shrugged it off and caught Jem a smart one on the shoulders. Now they were chest to chest, now they sprang apart, their breath whistling out of their mouths. Now they were in again, going like hammers, now they circled round looking for a way to each other's vitals. As the first round passed, the crowd went silent. They knew they were in for a real bout. As the two set on again, I saw my chance to complete the circle and get back to my friends. All around, the bets were being laid.

All the rivalries from the Merchants' Hall that morning had revived. Those for the Squire put their money on Daniel, those for Argent put their guineas on Jem. I began to see why Squire had been so agreeable to Argent. He reckoned to get his own back. All very well, I thought, if Daniel can stand the strain.

There was a roar as Jem staggered Daniel with a right cross on the jaw, but following up too close he got a taste of knuckle pie and spat blood. This brought a yell of rage from his supporters, but the cheers for both men were louder. Three rounds went by, four, five and in the middle the two of them fought on. The grass was trampled and slippery, they slid about as if they were on ice. Both were wet on the shoulders with sweat and blood. In each moment's silence their breath sounded harsh and quick.

Round ten came and went with a shout of "Fight on!" They fought on for I don't think they heard or cared.

By now they were beating each other senseless. Still they slogged on, toe to toe, hanging together like lovers, chins on each other's shoulders, mouths smeared with spit and blood.

It must have been by round twenty-one, or maybe twenty-two that to the crowd's fury and astonishment, the two backed off from each other and stood three paces apart, breath groaning in their throats, swaying and rocking on their feet. If a child had pushed them, they'd have dropped like stones. A draw by consent. I thought there'd be cheers for them both. They'd fought like heroes, no eye-gouging, no kicking, no kidney-punching. But no, someone in the crowd threw a clod and the cat-calls began again.

With more courage than I thought he had, Green-jacket jumped up and shouted,

"A draw, a good fight. Two great men well-matched."

There were cheers for that, and shouts of "No, Jem's fight." But Jem and Daniel didn't hear. Leaning on each other they struggled to the ropes and climbed out, while behind them the shower of clods and some stones, now, began to fall inside the ropes. The crowd began to sway and move like waves in the sea and to move downhill. I heard Mr Argent shout out to Green-jacket and that gentlemen, no doubt quaking inside, climbed through the ropes again. With him this time was a woman, gaunt and tall, clad only in her shift which she had belted round her waist like a man.

"Molly Brindle, Molly Brindle," came the roar.

"Molly Brindle," yelled Green-jacket, his voice cracked. "Molly Brindle challenges all comers."

Now Molly marched round the ring arms up, to the ribald comments of those nearest to which she replied with suitable gestures. Putting hands to her mouth she cried out.

"Any one of you, man, woman or in-between. Poor old Jem's worn out. But you won't beat Molly that easy."

The wagering which had drooped when Jem and Daniel withdrew, now revived, hotter and stronger. But where was the challenger? Gaunt Molly made one tour of the ring, gesturing more violently as if she hoped to enrage someone in the crowd to up and fight her.

"No."

The cry, though I did not know it, came from me. I saw the bonnet sail into the air, striking Molly in mid-oath and I knew, what few around me did, whose it was.

"No – don't."

But the next moment, Betsy, stripped to her scarlet shift, had pushed through the ropes and stood hand on hips in front of Molly.

"Who are you?" demanded Green-jacket.

"My name's Betsy!"

"Whose woman are you?"

"My own."

"Oho, her own?"

Molly spat. "Go home, girl, your mother wants you."

Betsy spat back.

"Old woman, go back to your spinning."

Back and to flew the insults, and before the crowd knew it the two had tucked their shifts up to their waist-belts and were at it. Now the wagers were laid fast and furious. I heard Squire call out.

"Well, Silver, my hundred guineas on Betsy. Will you put

yours on that old harridan?"

"Done," retorted Mr Argent.

The first fight had been slow and powerful, the second was quick and lively, Betsy and Molly exchanging insults between each blow. I winced as blows landed and turned my head away. The thought of Molly's brutal fists mangling Betsy's lovely flesh was too much to bear. But I'd no need to worry. Betsy was not there to suffer.

She side-stepped and slipped, ducked and dodged so lightly, Molly was at a loss. Once the older woman swung at the younger so powerfully it should have lifted Betsy's head off her shoulders if it had landed. It missed and the weight of it carried Molly on so violently, she sprawled on the grass while Betsy danced round her.

"Old woman, you're tired. Let me put you to sleep."

The crowd were muttering. This was not to their liking. Skill, agility were all very well, but what about the blood, and the solid thump of bone on flesh? As three more rounds went by like this, with only Molly growing slower and breathing harder as she chased Betsy round the ropes, the whistles and jeers began again.

"Stand and fight," shrieked one old girl. "Stand and fight." The cry was taken up and the pushing and swaying began again. Spectators pressed in so close that those nearest the fight were forced against the ropes and shouted for their fellows to give back and let them have room.

I heard one gentleman close to me mutter to his friend.

"If the old bitch doesn't land a blow soon, they'll riot."

He was right and wrong at the same time. Betsy led Molly in a tight circle on the flattened, greasy turf. Suddenly she dropped her fists. Molly crooked her elbow and drove on like a battering ram. Betsy was there no more, but a foot to the right. As Molly flew past, she drew up her hand like a pile driver and landed the older woman a colossal swipe under the ear.

In dead silence, Molly fell like a slaughtered ox and lay still with Betsy standing over her.

From the folk pressed up on the ropes only a pace or two away, rose the terrible cry:

"She's killed Molly Brindle."

—— 15 ——

Devil Take the Hindmost

"Molly's dead!" The news, true or false, passed from mouth to mouth, and the multitude of colliers, women and children were on the move. Those at the back pressed forward to see what was going on. Those in the middle pressed forward in their turn to get away from those behind them. Those at the front were flung forward as waves reach the beach when the tide is at the full. Thousands lurched over the turf in one huge surge.

"Molly's dead."

She wasn't. She was sitting up rubbing her jaw. Then she saw the great throng burst through the ropes and struggled to her feet. With Betsy heaving her along by the arm, she ran for safety just as the roped-in space was filled with bodies, running, stumbling, falling. Amid all the press, none could see she was alive. Amid all the clamour that she was dead, none could hear voices calling out that she wasn't. Green-jacket, his public duty done, took to his heels and, pushing ladies and gents to this side and that, he fled for the Three Feathers. Ned Barker suddenly appeared before us as the ladies and gentlemen disputed among themselves, calling out,

"Never mind your wagers, run for your lives."

Then he turned and with his mates linked arms and tried to hold back the crowd. It was like stopping the Severn at the bore with a plank, I thought, as I dived in quest of Betsy into the gentry who milled around like cattle. Those at the rear who had seen what was coming had prudently walked smartly, but with some dignity, towards their horses and carriages calling out nervously as they went. "Harness up, James, turn the carriage," and such instructions.

How much was heeded I can't say, for the servants, if they were not caught in the mêlée, were moving off to safer ground. Steps became strides, paces became a run. The cream of Bristol mercantile society broke into a trot, a canter and then a gallop, coat tails flying.

Skirts were hitched up to knees, then waists, well turned ankles, calves, thighs were displayed as they hurled themselves to waiting vehicles. Puffing and panting, hands clutching notes and sovereigns, or tragically spilling them to the ground, they ran for dear life with the welling tumult of the great crowd in their ears.

In vain Ned Barker and his fellows shouted for the colliers to halt and calm down. They were pushed to one side and the multitude moved on. Set in motion, none could now halt it. The distance between them and the fleeing gentry began to narrow. The sight of the quality in flight had an exciting effect on those in the van.

"Hey up, lads. There's Argent – the Engine man. There's his bloody inventor. Let's stuff 'em down the piston shaft," yelled one and the answer came, "Get the Engine man."

"Nay," came another cry, "get them that put the tollgates up last summer," and the response, "Aye, get the tollgate men."

And "Get them that put the corn up last year", "Aye get the badgers, get the 'grossers'."

With each repeated call the crowd began to split into separate trampling columns, a manoeuvre marvellous to see. I watched it from a corner of the Three Feathers which I reached. Being Little Tom had its advantages.

More wonderful to see; what divided the colliers, united the merchants. Forgetting they had ever fallen out on matters of State or religion, they fled as one man or one woman; Whigs along with Tories, Quakers and Methodists with High Church men, Free Traders and Tariff men, tollgate owners, corn chandlers, glass manufacturers, skippers, agents, speculators, enclosers, projectors, East India men, West India men, all ran close packed like a regiment of elite cavalry. Fell like a charge on the carriages, leaped through open doors, dived headfirst through windows, climbed like monkeys on roofs and driving seats.

Hurling grooms and coachmen aside, they seized reins and whipped up horses like regular Jehus. Converting a stately withdrawal into a desperate rout, they took the road to Bristol at a gallop. It had taken the better part of an hour to get out at noon. They came back at dusk in a handsome twenty minutes. First to his horse and leading the rout was the Recorder, ably accompanied by the Master of the Merchant Venturers'. Our party was mounted in the coach, with Daniel, bruised but recovered, on his seat, reins in hand.

"Where's Betsy?" I called to him. He did not seem to hear but set the horses on the road with a great cry and jerk of the leather.

"Betsy!" I yelled.

"Tom," said a voice behind me, and there she was, her white gown on, combing out her curly hair.

"Come, Betsy," I cried, and grabbing her by the hand, dragged her off as the verandah, floor and rail were turned to matchwood by trampling feet. Now we all ran together, for it was fatal to stop and I found Doctor Livesey at my side. He had missed the coach when he stopped to help a woman up from the grass. There was Ned Barker with Jem Morris at his side, face wiped clean but cuts and bruises showing fresh.

"Turn aside," shouted the Doctor to them. "You've done you're best. 'Tis not your fault what's happened."

"Nay, sir," gasped Barker. "I must keep up with the rest come what may, lest worse befall," and on he ran.

"The Recorder ran well," I jeered to the Doctor. He shook his head and puffed out, "Don't misjudge that gentleman. He's not run to save his skin, but to prepare a surprise packet for the colliers. I don't doubt 1 shall be needed tonight."

Before us the old walls of the city showed up, the setting sun behind them, filling the sky with a blinding glare. But dimly in the gap where the old gate had once stood I saw the constables drawn up, staves in hand, the Recorder on his horse and the Mayor at his side.

As the last lady and gent had passed through into safety, the constables plugged the gap.

"He's going to read the Riot Act," said the Doctor.

That might have been the intention but no word passed the Recorder's lips as the crowd over-ran constables and all, sending the Mayor flying over a hedge. Away went the Recorder on his horse like the wind.

What a man. He had another surprise packet in reserve. As the crowd stormed through the Lawford Gate and into the streets, the gentry dispersing before them, the setting sun shone on the sabres and muskets of the dragoons drawn up at one end of a square.

Betsy and I grabbed the Doctor by both arms and forced him through a narrow gateway into a garden at the side as we heard the first order to the soldiers.

We were over a wall on the far side of the garden when we heard the crash of the first volley.

The day's entertainment was over.

—— 16 ——

Jim Hawkins' Tale

Night fell. The colliers were in full flight out of the Lawford Gate, the dragoons in full cry after them. Our little party split up. Dr Livesey and Betsy went to the Guildhall to see what help might be given to the injured. I was sent by the Doctor to the house at the Hotwell to see how the rest of us had fared.

There was no cause for alarm. The Squire was sipping port by the window over the river. He'd spent an hour collecting gambling debts from those, including Mr Argent, who had rashly bet on poor Molly Brindle. He was delighted with Betsy. She was a jewel, a rare gift, he declared. He didn't know the half of it. He hadn't seen her thick as thieves with Mr A. And if I told him, would it make any difference? Not on your Sam. That morning he had sat in the Merchants' Hall, outraged and insulted. Tonight he sat in his house with his port, grinning all over his face and muttering, "Eight hundred guineas." He was not so hugely pleased with Daniel, but rewarded him with ten guineas. I suppose that was more money than Daniel had seen in his life. What he thought of it I couldn't say, for he couldn't tell me. I found him grooming the horses at the back. The cook had put goose grease on his cuts and he nodded to me without the flicker of an eyelid.

Back in the house the Doctor had come back with Betsy and he was having a glass with the Squire. For all the noise from the muskets, none, thank the Lord, had died. The soldiers had orders to fire over the heads of the crowd, and in any case said Dr Livesey, untrained troops always fire high. And he, having served in the French wars, ought to know. Betsy and he had treated a score of colliers whose heads were broken when the dragoons had laid into them with the flat of their sabres. And the town physicians had dealt with a dozen cases of hysteria among the gentlefolk at a guinea a time. But all the news was not so good.

Ned Barker and a handful of others, including Jem and Molly, who had tried to get the colliers out of the firing line had been arrested and would be charged with inciting to riot, etc.

Several gentlemen had testified to the Mayor that Barker had been heard to threaten Mr Argent with dire consequences and the crowd had been heard yelling, "Get the Engine man."

The Squire grunted: "True enough."

"If they testify so in court," added the Doctor, "these folk may hang or be transported."

"Well those who riot must be punished and those who incite to riot."

"Well, Mr Trelawney, sir," said the Doctor, drily, "if truth be known, some blame attaches to you."

"Me?"

"Aye, it all began in the boxing ring. You and your friends have done nicely out of it."

"Confound it, Livesey. How was I to know they'd take it like that? Bad sportsmanship."

"True, but that's not a hanging offence, or half the quality in this city would swing tonight."

Squire looked abashed at that.

"Well, what's to be done?"

"They'll come to no harm tonight," said Dr Livesey. "I've given the jailer the means to buy them supper. We'll wait to see what charges are brought, when tempers cool."

"Ah," said Trelawney, his mind back with his eight hundred guineas already.

"Meanwhile, there are the other charges," said the Doctor.

"Eh, what charges?"

"Those against you, Mr Trelawney, and myself and Jim; those gentlemen you took money off this evening are not going to forget us in a hurry."

"Pshaw," said Squire, "why that was just Silver – Argent's joke. All will be well, you'll see."

"Mr Trelawney!" I could see the Doctor was losing patience. "All will not be well. We have been accused, almost out of our own mouths, of every crime in the Newgate Calendar, before all the commercial gentry of Bristol. You may not care for that, but I do. I've laboured to build up the hospital for the poor and its welfare depends on the good will of such men."

"Confound it, Livesey," grumbled the Squire, "why must you always be in the right? I'm a hasty fool. What shall we do? That blasted lawyer Stilton or Wilton used Jim Hawkins' word against us. How can we answer that?"

The Doctor sat down quietly by the window and lit his pipe. For a while he smoked and looked out at the river below. Then he raised his head and pointed with his pipe stem.

"That's it, Trelawney. Tom, lad," he said to me, "go find Master Hawkins, if you please."

The next morning found us all assembled again in the Merchants' Hall. I had a sly look round at them all in their finery, and thought of them and their wives as they'd been yesterday, showing their plump rumps and heels to the world as they fought to come clear of the Kingswood colliers. One or two had the marks of the battle on their faces too. No doubt they would soon be telling the tale of how they'd fought off the mob to save their lady's honour. But that's the way of the world. This morning they were after other sport and here came Mr Argent, with Wensleydale and Stilton, ready to give it to them. Wilton carried a bundle of papers under his arm as usual. I was sure, though, that this was Mr Hawkins' story of the voyage to Treasure Island.

They must have lifted it on one of those visits to the Admiral Benbow. Tom Carter hadn't kept his eyes open wide enough. I felt bad about that for I owed it to Master Jim to look after his interests. He wasn't over clever in that respect. I looked at him where he sat next to the Doctor.

Doctor was whispering in his ear and he looked pale and concerned. This might well be, though, because he could see Lady Alice being greeted fulsomely by Mr A. and evidently liking it. I saw her chuckling over something he said, another gem of wit about his false leg, no doubt. I couldn't for the life of me see why Master Jim lost any sleep over her.

The Recorder was on his feet. "Gentlemen, and my Lady. We adjourned yesterday for the sake of calm reflection. We did not get it (laughter). All the same we must proceed. I take it, Mr Argent, that your case is complete?"

Mr Argent nodded genially.

"Then, Mr Trelawney, our attention is yours."

But it was Doctor Livesey who rose. "With your permission, sir, since I was one of that complement of the *Hispaniola* whose story you heard in snatches, mangled and distorted yesterday, I take the liberty of addressing you. I am not unknown in this city, nor is my work (there were nods at this) and I hope the gentlemen here will be as generous with their attention as they have been with their pockets in the matter of my charity." (A shrewd dig that, I thought.)

"My point is this. Yesterday you may have thought you heard the story of Treasure Island, because the written account was summarized and adorned so skilfully by Mr Wilton there. But, with respect, sir, that was not the book, that was simply a large review."

The Doctor turned to the company.

"How many of you gentlemen, having read a book, and then seen a so-called notice in a journal, have asked yourself – controlling your rage – the question: 'Has this reviewer even opened the pages of that book? I do not recognize it from what he writes'?"

Ah, he had them there and a good number, those who read the newspapers, laughed heartily.

"I will ask Mr Hawkins now to give us the full account, which I see Mr Wilton has under his arm, so that you may judge." He held out his hand. "If you will be so kind, Mr Wilton."

But Master Jim was on his feet.

"No need for that, Doctor. I know every line of it. Mr Wilton can confirm that not a word is out of place."

Old Stilton looked as if he'd object, but Mr Argent grabbed him by the arm.

"Let Mr Hawkins speak. He's the most honest man among us, I'll go bail for that."

So, Master Jim began his story. "Squire Trclawney, Dr Livesey, and the rest of the gentlemen having asked me to write down the whole particulars of Treasure Island . . ."

At first he was ill at ease and listeners were restless. But soon there was silence and everyone heard it as children attend to a story told before they sleep.

He told of the Admiral Benbow Inn, the dying old buccaneer, the blind man Pew, his terrible ways and his terrible death, the smiling sea-cook and his parrot, the island with its cliffs and pines, its beaches and swamps, its ambushes and hand to hand fighting, its deceptions and treachery, its delirium and death. And when he told of his lone fight with the coxswain Israel Hands aboard the *Hispaniola*, I no longer heard him. I was there, clinging to the cross trees, with a knife pinning my shoulder to the mast. I *was* Jim Hawkins and so was every creature in that hall.

Noon came but none was ready to adjourn. They sent out

for bread, meat and wine and brought Master Jim a great
tankard of ale to refresh him. Then the afternoon sun slowly
dwindled in the high windows.

"Shall we adjourn, gentlemen?" asked the Recorder.
"No, no," they cried. Candles were brought in and the tale
went on.

Only once did Master Jim pause in his story, when he told
of the quarrel among the crew, when a young sailor gave
Long John Silver the warning Black Spot. Mr Hawkins
fumbled in his pocket and held up a small scrap of paper.

"Here it is, gentlemen, cut from the last page of the Holy
Bible, by Mr Argent's old shipmate, Dick Johnson."

The lights had burned down and the room was almost
in darkness when he came to the words, "the worst dream
ever I have is when I hear the surf boom about its coasts,"
and repeated his oath never to see that island again.

For a moment or two the room was still, then as one person
they were on their feet, applauding, cheering. Some rushed to
shake his hand. More candles were brought in and the
Recorder got to his feet.

"Gentlemen. That was a privilege. How rarely can one
read such stories, these days, when so-called men of letters
fumble and finnick, split hairs and grub for this noun,
that adjective, and the reader is impatient for the tale to
begin.

"If ever a chronicle deserved publication, this is it."

Amid more clapping, he turned to Mr Argent.

"Now sir, is there some way in which you may be re-
conciled with these others who survived that terrible adventure? Surely for a man of your substance, that satisfaction
will be recompense enough for any past material loss, real or
imagined?"

"Hear, hear," they cried and one wit spoke up.

"From the many attentions, nay gallantries, I saw yesterday between Mr Argent and a certain person not uncon-

nected with Mr Trelawney, no doubt reconciliation is active already."

Mr Argent was on his feet, bowing to Lady Alice.

"I cannot imagine any more happy issue to this misunderstanding, than the regard of so elegant a lady, of such a fine family." He turned to Mr Trelawney. "After all, our families share Christian names, eh John, why not a share in a surname?"

How they admired that wit. How they roared. The Doctor shook his head in amazement. The Squire grinned.

Jim Hawkins marched up to Mr Wilton, took the papers from him and marched out. As he did so, the little curl of paper cut from the Bible fluttered to the floor. I nipped smartly across, picked it up and slipped it into my pocket.

Raisins and Wine

Only the Squire and Master Jim were at breakfast next morning. The Doctor was over at the jail visiting his "patients", Ned Barker and his party. Lady Alice was still abed. She took her breakfast when the sun had warmed the world a little.

Not a word was said at table. The Squire had drunk so many healths last night and the reconciliation suggested by the Recorder had gone on until the small hours. Master Hawkins, on the other hand, had gone to bed early. But he had nought to say, or perhaps he didn't trust himself to speak.

Outside, Daniel was harnessing the horses and the other servants made ready to close the house up. We were away home, our business done. The Master of the Merchant Venturers' had assured the Squire that the next Quarter Day would see him accepted "on the nod".

"Hanged if I see it at all," grunted Mr Trelawney, half to himself. "All that business Long John, or Mr Argent as he calls himself, started, unless . . ." he laughed so suddenly he clapped a hand to his aching head ". . . unless it was all a plot to court Lady Alice. Eh, Jim, maybe that was it. Ho! ho!"

Poor Master Jim stared out of the window. The Doctor came in briskly while the Squire was still laughing and wincing.

"What was that, sir?"

The Squire repeated his little joke and the Doctor, one

eye on Jim, hid his smile, then spoke seriously.

"I said we should watch Argent like a hawk – no, hanged if I see why I should call him by that fake French name. I knew our old friend was up to something. And I begin to see what it might be."

"What's that, then?"

"This. Silver has been to the Mayor and along with him to the jail. He has put down a bond of a thousand pounds for the colliers. They are bailed out on condition they sign to his personal service for seven years."

"Well, I call that generous. Better than transportation and a sight better than hanging," said the Squire.

"True. But there's talk about the wharves that he plans a sea voyage with the colliers as part of his complement. Since he can't want to give them the benefit of sea breezes for nothing, what is he up to?"

Squire looked pained with the labour of thinking.

"What are you driving at, Livesey?"

"Why, Squire, the bar silver buried under the Black Crag on the island. Who better than miners to dig it out? Who better to do his work than folk bound to him for fear of life and liberty? No chance of their crossing him."

Mr Trelawney shook his head. "Then what does he want with us? Why does he not set out? I don't see it, Doctor."

"Unless he's after the map, Mr Trelawney."

"The map – fiddlesticks. He knows where the cache lies."

"Ah," said the Doctor. "But can he place the island again, sir? Five square miles of rock and sand in thousands of square miles of blank sea."

"Oho," the Squire got to his feet, clutching at his forehead. "He's after the map is he? All that rigmarole to get the map. Well, we'll see about that. Come what may, that rascal (rascal again?) shan't have his hands on that map – or the bar silver."

He paced to and fro by the table.

"So that was the game, eh? Say, Jim, is the map in a safe place?"

But Master Jim did not seem to be listening. He was staring out of the window with a brooding look on his face.

"I'll warrant Jim's stowed that map where none may easily find it," put in the Doctor, sensing like I did that a small hurricane was brewing somewhere in the room.

"That's as maybe," said Squire. "But how did that fellow lay his hands on Jim's writings? They were stowed away were they not?"

He turned once more to Master Jim, making himself more agreeable.

"Might it not be as well to put it in a safe place, eh Jim? Say you were to bring it up to the Hall? Whatever else happens he must not lay his hands on that bar silver."

Abruptly Master Jim kicked back his chair and wiped his chin with a napkin. I could see his eyes were bright.

"You, sir, care very much that he should not lay his hands on the silver. But you don't seem to care that he makes free, in front of Bristol society, with Lady Alice's name. The money, sir, is all you care about. It is not so with me."

And with that out he went, leaving Squire speechless. The Doctor found something of great interest moving on the river and stared out of the window, whistling a small tune through clenched teeth.

Back we rode from Bristol that day. I sat cheek by jowl and hip to hip with Betsy up above, while my master rode below respectably next to Lady Alice. I know who had the more pleasant journey. As he played with the rein in his great black hands, Daniel sang a funny song in that deep outlandish voice of his.

"What's he singing?" I asked Betsy, but she only answered, "Mind your own business."

At the Hall, the Squire got down and bid me wait behind

a while, sending the coach on to take the Doctor and Master Jim home. On the pretence of asking me for advice over wine, he led me into the library and with a heavy wink bid me be seated. Then he poured out a glass of port apiece.

"Raisins, Tom. Will you have raisins?"

I shook my head. Port at this hour of the day was quite enough.

"Funny. Master Jim always found raisins most acceptable."

"No accounting for taste, sir."

"Tom, lad. Let's talk, man to man. We are both fond of your master. A truer man never stepped."

I drank to that.

"A touch tender on matters of principle."

Amen to that, too.

"See, Tom. I'm worried. 'Twixt you and me and the mainmast, Master Hawkins don't give tuppence whether that rogue, Silver or Argent, gets his greedy hands on the bar silver. Well, I do." He looked cunning at me. "And I'll wager my best brace of pistols, so do you."

"Sir!"

"You and I must see to it that that map does not fall into the wrong hands. And we must do it without giving offence to Master Hawkins."

I nodded. "You want me to pinch it and bring it to you at the Hall?"

He looked shocked. "No, no, no, Tom. Don't be hasty. What I want is for you to keep your eyes peeled. I'll make it worth your while."

"Sir, you're already paying me well enough as it is."

"Eh, what's that? Paying you? Don't get your drift, lad."

Oh ho, I thought. That monthly shilling I was getting via Betsy, wasn't from the Squire. But who, then? Argent? The world was spinning a bit too fast for me.

"I only meant to say, sir, you've been kindness itself. Treated me handsomely."

"I'll do more for you, Tom." He leant over and dug me in the ribs. "What do you think of Betsy, eh?"

I must have blushed somewhat for he roared with laughter.

"Well, then. If all goes well, perhaps you shall have her to wife, that's if a wench like that understands marriage."

"If I thought she would, sir . . ."

"What, Tom? We shan't ask her. We know what's what, don't we?"

He dug me in the ribs again and bid me pour him another glass.

— 18 —

Some Like it Hot

At the Admiral Benbow we went about our business. That is to say, I looked after the inn and the custom. Mrs Hawkins sat guard with her sewing and her pistol. And Master Jim went back to his pen-chewing at the table. He'd paid some heed to opinion and given up playwriting. Now he was busy writing a romance called *The Prince of the Indies*, which, 'twixt you and me, was his old play turned into prose. But the customers liked the new arrangement better, for least ways he did not make them join in playreading at nights. He laboured alone, only now and then, late at night, asking me to listen while he read a chapter or two. Hard going it was, too.

Time and again, it was on the tip of my tongue to ask him about that other story he'd told in Merchants' Hall, or about that round, yellowed scrap of paper cut from the buccaneer's Bible, which I had stowed in my fob pocket. But since I'd picked that up without his knowing, I thought I'd better keep mum about it. Most of all I'd have liked to know where that map was hidden. I'd my suspicions about a squeaking floorboard under his bed, but got no chance to investigate. Other people, of course, were interested in the map, too.

Twice Betsy came down to the inn with dinner invitations from the Hall. The Squire was doing all he could to butter Master Jim up. But he excused himself. He was unwell, or Mrs H. had had a turn (that was a joke, for the Old Lady might not know who her son was, but that apart, she was as sound as a bell, as she was soon to show us).

So Squire sat and fumed with impatience at the Hall. Master Jim sat and brooded and chewed his pen down at the Admiral Benbow. Betsy flitted to and fro, and the Doctor called by now and then for a chat, looking somewhat careworn.

"Hang the treasure," he said to me, once. "It kills friendship and friendship's all that matters."

Amen to that, I thought, but a little treasure wouldn't go amiss for those who had nought.

No doubt Mr Argent thought so to, but he was biding his time. He stayed away from our parts or seemed to do. And perhaps he had no need, with Betsy nosing around on his behalf.

Try as I might, I couldn't make out where that map might be. At the least, I'd have liked to have a look at it, out of curiosity. One day when Master Jim was down at the cove, looking out to sea, I gave his bedroom the once over, and then the twice over. But not a sign of any map. The squeaky floorboard was not to be moved and I could find no hiding place. The bundle of papers with the story written on them, was in a canvas wrapping under the bed and that was all.

One evening, a quiet one in the tap, we sat in the parlour, Master Jim writing, Mrs H. sewing and me thinking of this and that, when the old lady nodded off. One of her pistols slipped from her lap with her sewing and hit the deck with a thump. But it didn't fire, which was a miracle, because she was in the habit of keeping 'em cocked. As I picked it up I noticed there was no wadding. But before I could look at it more closely Mrs H. woke up and snatched it back from me.

I saw them both looking my way.

"That one ain't loaded, Tom," said Mrs Hawkins in a tone

of voice which meant "Mind your own business." Now what did that mean? I wondered.

It wasn't long before I found out.

That very next day, in the early evening, before we'd opened up, the old lady was sitting by the range in the kitchen. Master Jim was up aloft and I was busy in the tap. A storm had been brewing up all day and the sky outside was overcast with thick purple clouds. It was so dark that I lit a lamp or two. There was a rumble of thunder out to sea and a flicker of lightning now and then. We were in for a dirty night and I wondered if the rain would come before our regulars arrived.

Suddenly Mrs H. looked up and said in a queer voice, "What's that, Jim, lad?"

I heard the tap of a stick on the road outside. It drew nearer and nearer. The old lady seemed to be holding her breath, her eyes staring. The look on her face put my heart in my mouth. The sound came nearer and nearer. Then it struck sharp on the inn door and we could hear the handle being turned and the bolt rattling as someone tried to get in. I moved to open the door, but she whispered,

"Don't go, Jim. Don't let him in."

There was a long silence, then the tapping died away. I went to the window and peered out. At that moment there was a lightning flash, a clap of thunder. The yard, the road and the cliff heads were lit up. But there was no one to be seen, though in the distance I thought I heard the sound of coach wheels.

Now the storm got into its stride. The rain came down in sheets banging on the windows and running in streams from the roof. Ever hopeful, I made all ready in the bar and went through into the parlour where I sat with Master Jim and waited for the first customers. But none came.

After an hour the rain eased up as swiftly as it had begun, though the sky did not clear for the dusk of evening was adding to the gloom. In the silence that came after the downpour all three of us heard that tapping again. Closer it came right up to the threshold. The door latch clicked and slow steps sounded in the tap.

"Who's that?" called Mrs Hawkins from the kitchen. At the same time, Master Jim who had been listening open-eyed as though he didn't believe what he heard, jumped to his feet and strode into the tap.

A whispered conversation now began. I could not hear what was being said, so got to my feet and went to the curtain. Beyond the lamp light near the outer door, I saw two figures: Master Jim and the mysterious visitor. They were arguing and the disagreement grew fiercer. Of a sudden I heard: "The map? You shall not have the map."

"No, indeed he shan't," screamed Mrs H. There was a scuffle, a table turned over. I pushed aside the curtain in time to see the old lady rush into the tap and empty a big pot of pease pudding over the intruder's head. I daresay Master Jim got a helping, too, for he staggered to one side. Mrs Hawkins ran past me into the parlour and back into the tap where Master Jim was picking himself up and the other man was tottering blindly through the outer doorway. The old lady had the pistol in her hand.

"Don't shoot, Mrs Hawkins," I called. But that wasn't her plan. Instead, she thrust the pistol into my hand. I could tell from the weight, it was the empty one.

"Take it, Tom, lad. Run to Squire or Dr Livesey with it. They shan't have it."

I rushed out past the stranger with his head-dress of warm pease pudding and headed for the road and down to the little bridge that carried it over a stream nearby. Over the brow of the hill I could hear horses galloping. As I ran for it the intruder stopped his bellowing and got words out.

"Help! Jim! Tom! Don't leave me!"

It was Squire. I knew that voice even through two pounds of pease pudding. Back to the road I climbed to meet him as he came tumbling down towards the stream. But in that moment the noise of horses topped the rise and four or five riders came in sight in the moonlight and swept at full gallop down the slope.

The Squire saw his error, turned with a roar and ran straight for the ditch into which he rolled. But he was on his feet again in a second and making another dash now utterly bewildered right under the nearest of the coming horses.

As he did, the rider put out a foot and deftly tipped him head over heels back into the ditch. At the same time a voice said in my ear: "Jump up, Tom."

I was seized by my belt, hauled up and was astride the horse's rump in an instant.

My seat was anything but secure and I had to cling on for dear life to the coat of the man I rode pillion to, for we went off at a spanking pace. Half a mile up the road I found my voice.

"Where are we going?"

"Shut your mouth," came the helpful answer. The troop did not slacken its pace for two miles and more when all turned aside on a narrow track, rode a couple of hundred yards over grass and reined up outside a big lonely house. With no more delay, I was hauled off my mount, pushed inside the front door and up a broad flight of stairs. As we went, my hand brushed the banisters. They were thick with dust. Upstairs, a door was opened and I was shoved inside a large, well-lighted room.

Down the centre was a table, covered in white cloth and tastefully laid with silver for two. Our arrival was well-timed for the soup was steaming on the table and the first wine poured. Behind the table, between the two tallest candlesticks, stood a tall, stoutly built man, in blue broad-skirted coat with a cocked hat on his head. On his shoulder sat a mangy and ageing green parrot. His other shoulder was supported by a crutch on which he leaned lightly. As I reached the table, he hopped dexterously forward, took his place neatly and laid aside the crutch.

"Come aboard, Tom," said Mr Argent.

Wine without Raisins

"Sit down, Tom. Here's your health, shipmate."

I tasted the wine. It was good. The soup was pretty fair, too. I was hungry. The fresh air sharpened my appetite. Mr Argent didn't eat. He talked instead.

"I can see you're a lad after my own heart, such as I might have been proud to have as my own son, though so far as I know, I've no children, more's the pity."

So far as I knew, he might be my own Dad, for that gentleman had left my mother as soon as he loved her. Anyone walking about might be my Dad, and me none the wiser. I ate my soup and they brought in the roast, a mite too quickly perhaps, but then maybe he was short of time.

"You and I have to talk, get things ship-shape and Bristol fashion," said Mr A., though having seen a bit of Bristol fashion I didn't quite know how to take that.

"Most of all, shipmate, you put me in mind of Jim Hawkins when we two shipped aboard the *Hispaniola*. Hang it, why does one have to get old, Tom, lad? Look at me." He pulled off his wig. "Bald as a coot."

Just then, who should come in but old Wensleydale, carrying Mr Argent's false leg. He barely nodded to me, but spoke to Argent with excitement in his voice.

"See that, Mr Argent?"

He held up the leg and worked it to and fro at the knee, so that the foot shot out and narrowly missed his patron's head.

"That, sir, is a ball and socket joint, designed by me and

made by a local craftsman. Not an imitation of Nature, sir, but an improvement thereon. The principle is the ball bearing, solid spheres of metal, like pistol shot, encased in grease or wax." He jerked the leg again, holding it away from Mr Argent, so that the toe swept a water carafe from the table. "Properly turned to the needs of industry, why, sir, this would transform motive power.

"The application of reason makes possible the . . ."

Argent jerked the leg out of the Inventor's hand and hurled it across the room.

"Sling your hook, Somerscale. I'm in no mood for reason tonight," he snapped. Somerscale slung his hook, but looked ill-pleased. It seemed to me that Mr Argent might one day regret the way he treated the Inventor.

"Look at me, Tom, an old hulk on a lee shore. Look at the old parrot, Cap'n Flint, that sailed with England, that's seen Providence, Portobello and the Tortugas, that's learnt every word, good or bad, a sailor or gent of fortune could wish to know. See the state she's in."

At this the parrot opened its beak and screamed. "Ten per cent, ten per cent. Take it or leave it."

Argent shook his head. "She's changed for the bad. After all these years in business I can't get a civil, human word out of her, but ten per cent. Ah, Tom, lad, I've led a bad life."

"But that was years ago you quit the sea, Mr Argent."

"Nay, Tom, since then, since then. I used to kill 'em swift and painless, a knife in the guts, a cutlass blade across the throat. These days I bleed 'em to death and they thank me for it."

"All except Ned Barker and his mates," I said.

He grinned.

"Even Ned Barker eats out of my hand now. The shade of the gallows cools the hottest brow. But, hang it, we shan't speak of such, shall we? Tom, lad. If I could just get my feet on the deck, why I'd rig up my old line and hop about like a cricket. Off I'd sail to Treasure Island and lift that bar silver. No hang it all, it's not the treasure, it's the glory of the sea."

"You sound powerful like Squire Trelawney."

"There's a gentleman now. Hasty in temper but a British bulldog through and through. Once he gets his teeth in, he never lets go. I'll wager he'd be off to Treasure Island if he could."

"So he would," I answered, "though he's strapped for the ready. What holds you back, sir?"

"Why, what a sharp 'un you are, little Tom, and no mistake. No, it's not the funds that hold me back. 'Tis, well 'tis the map."

"But, Mr Argent, you know that island like the back of your hand, moorings and all, so Mr Hawkins said."

"So I do, so I do. But where is the blessed spot, now you tell me? I can fit out a ship and sail west. But I might sail till kingdom come and never make landfall. It's latitude and longitude, that fails me, Tom, naught else." He leaned towards me.

"Tom, lad. Throw in with me. I know you can get the map, if you set your mind to it."

He didn't know how near the mark he was.

I shrugged. "If I get you the map, now, you share the treasure with me, later. Where's the bargain?" I grew bolder. "See, Mr Argent, five guineas down and a shilling a month don't buy me lock, stock and barrel."

"Shilling a month, shilling a month, what bilge is that?"

He stared at me. Where did that blessed shilling come from then? Somebody was playing double with me. He looked cunning.

"I can offer you something better. Your freedom."

"What freedom?"

He snapped his fingers. In the doorway appeared two men. I groaned to myself. The bounty hunters again.

"So they were in your pay all the time?"

"Not so, Tom, lad. They joined my little party 'cause it paid 'em. And it'll pay you. I'll share pirate fashion with you, Jim, none of your blessed gentlemen's legal ways. That'll mean thirty thousand pounds – depending," he went on hastily, "what silver fetches on the market. You get the map, I pay off these lads here and off we sail to the west."

"That's no bargain," I protested.

"Take it or leave it," screeched Cap'n Flint and stretched out her threadbare wings. Out of the corner of my eye I measured the distance to the outer door. Could I reach it before the two villains at the other end of the room?

"Your health, Mr Argent," I said, lifting my glass and tipping it in his friendly, smiling mug. As he spluttered, I made a dash for it. But I'd misjudged speed and distance. A yard from the door I felt that familiar hand on my collar. Argent wiped his face.

"I take that hard, Tom, lad," he said, and there was a chilling sound to his voice. This man cut throats to get his way. I walked back to the table but the hand stayed on my collar.

"Now, Tom, let's start again. Where's the map?"

Before I could answer the outer door crashed open. In the doorway was Master Jim, his mother's two pistols in his hands.

"Over here, Tom, look lively." I did. I skipped for the door while the three of them stared. Then one made a move.

"I don't advise it," said Mr Argent. The villain stopped.

"Jim, lad, come aboard. I call it handsome of you to pay us a visit."

Master Jim did not speak, but reversed one of the pistols in his hand. Taking it by the barrel he threw it on the table.

"The map's inside the barrel, Silver. It's yours if you sheer off and leave us in peace. If not . . ."

"Well, Jim, if not . . ."

Master Hawkins raised the second pistol.

"Then you get what's inside this barrel." He turned to me. "Come, Tom, lad, let's go home."

—— 20 ——

Silver's Revenge

Outside on the grass two horses were grazing. I recognized them as we mounted. They were Squire's coach horses. Master Jim laughed.

"Daniel has two left to take the Squire back to the Hall, now Mother's finished cleaning him down. That's the last time he'll call secretly."

We set off without more ado and were well down the road when I remembered to ask about the map.

"I found it where you hid it," said Master Jim, "under the bridge. Then I followed as quick as I could."

Twenty minutes' steady trot brought us to the Admiral Benbow. We'd no fear of pursuit now Argent had the map. Giving it to him had taken a weight off my master's mind and he whistled as he rode along. At the inn we found Ben Gunn in the doorway, tankard in hand.

"Good evening to you, Jim, lad, and little Tom. And, says you, what's Ben Gunn doing here? And I says, Squire bids Master Hawkins and young Tom come up to the Hall, quick as you can. Great matters afoot, that's what." He struck the side of his nose with his finger.

We set the horses going again and reached the Hall soon enough, where Daniel took them to the stables and Betsy led us straight into the library. Everyone was there, Squire, Doctor, Lady Alice. And standing near the fire was a tall, broad-shouldered man in skipper's garb, someone I'd never seen before. Master Jim knew him, right enough, for he called out,

"Captain Gray," and gave him his hand.

So that was Gray. I remembered Abraham Gray, the carpenter's mate, from Master Jim's story, the man who'd swapped sides and helped win the treasure. Now a captain, eh?

"Good to see you, Jim. And who's this?"

"Tom Carter, my assistant at the Admiral Benbow."

"Worth his weight in gold, too," said the Squire.

"What brings you here, Abraham?" asked Jim. "We would have welcomed you at Merchants' Hall a month back, I can tell you. Your word would have clinched the matter."

Gray laughed. "From all that Doctor tells me I think your word carried weight enough, Jim, lad. As to why I'm here now, best ask Squire."

This was Mr Trelawney's cue. He could not have held his peace a moment longer.

"Jim, Tom, come take a glass of wine. Raisins, Jim? Not for you, Tom, I know. Sit you down."

We sat and Squire rattled on.

"First, your pardon, Jim, that I took you off guard tonight. I wanted to come to you discreet and confidential you understand. But that blasted map set us at odds. But, see, while you've been at your business, I've been at mine. Aye, and our good friend Blandly has been busy. He's found me the means of borrowing more ready money. He's found me a crew, and today he sent me a captain, not just a captain, but *the* captain."

"Captain?" said Jim, making out to be baffled. "For what?"

"For the ship. Come, Jim, you can't keep up this nonsense any longer, not when you hear my next news."

"What is that, sir?"

"Why the ship, Jim, the blessed ship. Blandly's found the *Hispaniola* again, laid up, but seaworthy still, used for the fishing trade. She's at a jetty down at the mouth of the Avon.

She can be fitted out and not a soul in Bristol any the wiser. Ha, we won't make the mistake we made last time. A hand-picked crew, paid double for the voyage. We pay 'em off in Kingston, work the ship over to the island ourselves. Daniel and the others will raise the bar silver for us and we'll be home by Michaelmas." He paused. "Home before Silver even knows the game's up."

"But, Squire," said Jim, his face with a thunderstruck look on it.

"Don't interrupt me, Jim. There's more, lad, more. Wensleydale – you know the Inventor fellow . . . He's ready to finish with Silver. Treats him abominably. He'll come in with us and keep us informed what Silver is about, so we can forestall him. All he wants is a little capital for a new project of his. So now, Jim, all we need is for you to bring the map and show us the way."

"Mr Trelawney," shouted Jim, in desperation as though he were drowning in the words that tumbled out of the Squire's mouth. "The map!"

"The map, what of it? You have it safe; Tom took it tonight from Mrs Hawkins and hid it. A rare lad is Tom, just the sort to be cabin boy, as you were, I'll wager."

Master Jim's voice sank.

"I gave the map to Silver."

"You did what?" Squire, Doctor, Lady Alice, Captain Gray, all sang out on different notes like a quartet in the opera.

"Aye," he answered defiantly. "I gave it to him. How else do you think I rescued Tom? Tom's a wanted lad and Silver was handing him over to the bounty hunters."

"Bounty hunters," said Lady Alice scornfully. "I know why you gave him the map. You wanted to get rid of him . . . and all because he paid me the compliment of a little attention."

"But he's old enough to be your father."

"He's a man of mature years, 'tis true."

"He's a false leg."

"He's sound in other respects."

"He's a murdering pirate."

"You're a bad playwright."

The last blow hit Master Jim below the belt. But she'd not done yet.

"If I choose to, I'll marry Mr Argent and sail with him. Why should I not, now he has the map?"

And with that broadside hitting Master Jim amidships, out she sailed, slamming the door behind her. I wondered if Betsy had managed to jump clear. But my lady had made such a din they could hear her all over the house.

Poor Master Jim looked sick and no mistake. The Squire and Captain Gray stared into the fire. The Doctor tapped out his pipe on the fireplace and turned calmly to Master Jim.

"Why, Jim, this night, you've taken fifteen years off me."

"He's added fifteen to me," growled the Squire.

"I remember," went on Dr Livesey, "how on that fateful voyage, time after time, by your rash actions you plunged us all into peril, yet at the same time by some stroke of fortune, rescued us again. Not a whit have you changed. Act first, reflect later, that's Jim Hawkins' way."

Master Jim looked ashamed, then lifted his chin. "I did what I thought right. I was against the treasure quest from the start and I did intend to rid us of that man."

"Jim," said Dr Livesey, "for your feelings on the treasure I respect you. For your feelings towards Silver, I applaud you. But, if the motive of it all was love of Lady Alice, then permit me to call you an ass."

"An ass?"

"Aye, freely. You are not the first to think he can win a lady against her will by driving away the rival. You will not be the last. But it works only in a contrary fashion. It insults her and dishonours you."

The Doctor took his glass and drank, then addressed the company.

"What's Silver after – treasure? The Lady Alice? Maybe, but whatever it might seem to be there's one word for it – revenge. He humiliates the Squire in front of Bristol traders, impudently hints at marriage to his ward, no doubt planning to outlive him and come to lord it in this Hall, sitting by this fireplace." Squire looked green at that. "And you, Jim, will let him have the bar silver and throw Lady Alice into his arms for good measure."

The Squire leaped to his feet, regardless of his bandaged leg. "We'll daddle him yet. We'll off to sea in the *Hispaniola* and take the bar silver from under his nose."

"He's got the map," warned the Doctor.

"So much the worse for him. We've got a ship ready for sea, and Jim knows the cross-bearings by heart or I'm a Dutchman. Let's cut and run for it. Tom shall come with us and be safe from the bounty hunters and no questions asked. Why the vessel's nearly ready to sail. We could have stores and all on board in two days. See here, Jim, I've thought of everything. My cook shall go down and lodge with your mother and see her right. Doctor's hospital can shift for itself for a while. What d'you say, Jim?"

"But . . ."

"Don't fret for Lady Alice. She'll be on board with us, you'll see. She's no fool. In with us, she gets her share and mine when I go. Married to Silver, I leave everything to Livesey's blessed infirmary. She'll get naught from me and naught from him, and she knows it."

Well, thought I, a smart about turn and no mistake.

Squire had his glass up. "What's it to be?" he asked.

Jim sat a moment in thought, then with a sigh he raised his glass. Everyone cried:

"The *Hispaniola*."

PART

— 3 —

My Sea Adventure

———————

The Hispaniola

The next two days went by like a whirlwind. With the Squire pushing and Captain Gray overseeing, our preparations for the voyage went swiftly and secretly. No one left the Hall, and with mixed feelings I kept a close eye on Betsy. If she wanted to warn Silver, she got no chance. Our advance party took the main stores and gear down that first night. On the second, the rest of us set out in pitch darkness with masked lanterns. On the long journey to the mouth of the Avon, along the winding coastal road, which in some places was no better than a track, we were joined in great secrecy, by Somerscale the Inventor.

With a glint in his eye he showed us a small cloth bundle. He opened it to show half a dozen small metal spheres.

"My invention. Without this he can't move more than a yard without his leg seizing up." Mr Argent, he assured us, was unaware of what we were doing and was making his own preparations for his voyage. But could not be ready for at least a week.

The Squire was delighted, like a boy who has played a trick and got away with it. And when we reached the jetty at the river mouth, a lonely place of mud flats and weed beds and a few broken down cottages, and found the battered old schooner moored there, he was ready to burst with pride. He was first to run up the narrow plank on to the maindeck and before any other business could be done he had to show us how smart he'd been with the fitting out.

"They won't catch us napping again," he declared. "See,"

121

he pointed to the stern, "arms and powder stored aft below the rear cabins. Over the cabin roof, a second swivel gun, firing grape shot. Just let anyone try a mutiny. And 'midships, see . . ."

"An apple barrel?" cried Master Jim.

"An apple barrel, Jim, lad, just to remind us all that plotting don't pay. All fair, square and above board on this trip."

It was then near sunset and our gear was safely stowed. Below decks we went to our quarters.

The crew was as small as Captain Gray dared make it and every man aboard was expected to take his watch. We ate supper together, drank another toast to the voyage and then went to our hammocks with the Squire's words in our ears.

"Up at crack of dawn. We sail on the morning tide."

I woke in the half dark to the sound of shouting. I stared round me in the small space I shared aft with Master Jim. His hammock was empty. Overhead I heard feet tramping up and down. The ship was lifting gently as the tide rose. They were getting ready to sail and I was still abed.

In haste I pulled on my breeches, tucked in my shirt and ran for the companion way, knocking my head sharply on a beam as I went. I'd yet to learn to fit into my new floating home. Out on deck I came, in the grey dawn light. No sign of the sun yet, but a breeze pulling at the small spread of canvas which was creeping up the masts. I looked around me. Folk were running to the port side and gathering by the rail where the gang plank still linked us to the shore.

Sailors in the act of casting off were standing stupidly staring, ropes in hand. At the head of the gangway, his face purple, his eyes bulging, stood the Squire. Next to him stood Captain Gray, looking bewildered.

"Cast off," yelled the Squire.

"Nay, heave to," came a familiar jovial voice from the

jetty. "Make way for the owner."

Owner?

I rushed to the side and clambered into the ratlines to see what was afoot. And I nearly pitched headfirst into the water 'twixt ship and land.

For there on the jetty, standing by a baggage waggon, were Ned Barker, Jem Morris, Molly Brindle and two other colliers. Behind them stood Wilton-Stilton the lawyer with his papers under his arm.

And behind him, large as life and twice as cheerful, was Mr Argent.

—— 22 ——

Walking the Plank

"By gor, he never gives up."

Standing by me at the ship's rail, rubbing sleep from his eyes was old Wensleydale, staring down at Mr Argent and his partner.

"Mr Somerscale, sir," I said. "Taking his ball bearings hasn't made any difference."

He looked peeved at that, but said, "You wait and see, my lad."

I did. It was the most you could do where Mr Argent was concerned. The two opposing forces, one on the ship, the other on land were still for a moment, sizing one another up. I expected Squire to give the order to "repel boarders". But Jem Morris spoiled the grandeur of the occasion by spotting Daniel at the rail and giving him the thumbs up sign.

"Owner?" called the Squire. "What the devil's this?" He turned to the crew. "Cast off," he shouted.

"Hold hard," yelled Argent, and they dropped the ropes again. There was something about him that made folk do as he said. Mr Wilton plucked a paper from under his arm and held it up.

"The 300-ton schooner, *Hispaniola*, registered in Bristol?"

"You know damn well it is."

"Master, Captain Abraham Gray?"

Cap'n Gray leaned over the rail. "What's your business, sir? We must cast off now or we'll lose the tide."

"Hirer, Mr John Trelawney?"

The Squire could stand no more. "What's all this rigmarole?" said he, putting his foot on the plank.

"Your hire, sir," intoned old Stilton, reading from his papers, "is conditional on reserving place for the owner and party, if he should desire passage in his own ship."

"What of it?"

"Owner, John Argent."

"He – " the Squire took his foot off the plank and leaned on the rail for support "... can't be. Blandly told me nothing of that."

Argent smiled, and came slowly and stiffly up to the gang plank.

"Mr Blandly's the soul of discretion."

"He's a conniving blackguard," said the Squire. I saw the Doctor, who watched the whole scene from the foredeck, hide a smile.

"Hang it, Silver. Get your own ship. You have the map." Squire sounded more in sorrow than in anger.

Mr Argent shook his head regretfully. "I've been thinking about that map. I remember once before, fifteen years ago, one of your party gave me a map, a man otherwise the soul of honesty. And it wasn't worth a brass farthing. So I thought, I musn't let them play the same trick again, not at my age. So, I fear we'll all have to shove up a bit and make room. We've brought our own provender, never fear. And, in consideration, I'll share the hire of the ship, after we've divided the bar silver."

As he spoke he was climbing slowly up the plank, his false leg playing tricks with him. He was half way there when he reached the words "bar silver" and they acted on Squire like a match to a cannon touch hole. He rushed down the plank to meet Mr Argent, shouting, "Cast off" as he went, and such was the effect of this sudden command that the men at the ropes paid out enough, what with the tide and the wind, to make the ship stir and shift. Just as Squire and Mr Argent were nose to nose, the plank tilted and down they went almost in each other's arms, into two fathoms of muddy water 'twixt hull and jetty.

"Man overboard," shouted Mr Hall, the mate, which wasn't strictly correct. Men started to run to and fro on deck and shore. Lady Alice cried out.

Who she screamed for I don't know. But she didn't faint like a regular lady, but whipped up her skirts and scrambled up in the ratlines like a matelot, to see the fun, just as two great gouts of water shot up by the ship's side. Daniel and Ned Barker had dived in, one from the jetty, t'other from the ship and now there were four of them rising and falling and churning up the mud.

Up came the Squire wearing a cap of slime on his bare head, spitting out water and yelling "Cast off." Down he went and up came Mr Argent, with his "Heave to." Up shot Ned Barker, holding Argent's false leg in his hand which had come off in the struggle. He cast it aside in disgust and plunged down again. Up came Daniel, the Squire in his arms, not just saving him but keeping him from strangling Mr Argent. But the Squire broke free, just as Ned Barker and Mr Argent surfaced. Now it was free for all with Mr Argent and Squire grappling, and Daniel and Ned Barker pulling 'em apart, up and down, in and out, like a mad quadrille. How long it might have gone on I can't say, but Captain Gray took charge, had a loading net lowered and fished them up like outsize mackerel, dumping them on deck, running water and seaweed, Mr Argent holding his false leg and Squire clutching his wig.

Not a moment too soon, Captain Gray ordered them all below for blankets and brandy, bid those on shore make haste and pack aboard with their gear and gave orders to cast off without delay. This time there were no more delays and thanks to British seamanship and skill, we caught the tide and spun merrily out to sea.

I went below in case I was needed. The swimming party had changed their clothes. Squire and Argent were wrapped in blankets and half way down a bottle of brandy. Good humour was the order of the day, believe it or not.

"When we get there, John, I may call you John, eh," said Mr Argent, "I'll race you for the bar silver."

"Hmph. You've your false leg."

"Aye, but my mechanic's gone over to your side."

"Much good he's done me so far."

"Ah, John, it'd take more than a few ball bearings to stop this old salt."

I left 'em to it and went on deck. With fair winds we were soon out of sight of land, and the schooner rose and fell with the kind of regular motion that will turn your guts inside out if you're not used to it. There is only one cure for mal de mer, so Old John the journeyman, who served with the navy, told me, and that is occupation.

I went below in the galley. In the haste of departure no one had been named cook, so I thought I'd set to. I found Molly Brindle down there and we got along like a house on fire. We split the work between us. She had a rare touch with the rough stuff, my stronger point was for the delicacies. And if, during the voyage, with the ship swaying and dipping and the pots and pans skating here and there, sometimes things got mixed up, and the best quality meat went to the fo'c'sle and the stuff from the knacker's yard went to the officer's quarters, then, there's justice under heaven and a good sauce, as the French can tell you, hides a multitude of sins. In a word Molly and I got on and everyone on board got the benefit.

The ship settled down for a long voyage. But not without a few little troubles. On the second day out at sea, Mr Hall noticed some hands were shifting the arms and powder to starboard.

"Hold hard," says he. "Who's told you to do that?"

"Owner's orders," came the answer.

That afternoon he found them shifting the arms and powder back to port.

"Hirer's orders," was the word.

Then there was pushing and shoving over quarters. With seven extra bodies on board and three females in the company now with variation of race and degree to say nothing of religion. Well it might have come to blows and brawling. But Abraham Gray was not having that. He called Mr Argent and the Squire to his cabin and asked me to bring up some wine. Then he set about them, politely.

"Two crews, two employers. It won't do, gentlemen. Not when both of them are in their sixties and behaving like schoolboys."

He thumped on the table.

"If it doesn't stop, I'll exercise my rights as captain to return to port and set you both ashore."

That cooled them down. Then he gave his instructions about quarters. Crew forward, servants and hired labour amidships and the rest aft, with canvas screens put up for the privacy of the women. We didn't know how useful that was to prove later on.

Once the shifting round was done, on the fourth day out, the ship settled down to a steady six knots, the crew to their work and everyone else to their own concerns.

"Well, Tom," said Squire, "we sorted that out easily enough."

"Aye aye, sir," I answered.

"Then it's ho for Treasure Island," said Squire.

But Ben Gunn met me on the deck and muttered to me, tapping the side of his nose with his finger.

"Now, Tom, lad, I asks you, how many have we got on board? and you says, right away, twenty-six. And I says to you, that's the same number as sailed aboard the *Hispaniola* last time. And I asks you, how many came back? Tom, how many came back?"

And without waiting for an answer, off he skipped.

── 23 ──

The Apple Barrel

We had some heavy weather which only proved the qualities of the old *Hispaniola*. Every man and woman on board seemed well content and they must have been hard to please if they had been otherwise for it is my belief that never was a ship's company so spoiled since Noah put to sea.

In the galley, with Molly Brindle, I turned out everyone's fancy, rack of lamb, hot pot, dumpling, red pea soup, shepherd's pie. Double grog was served on suitable occasions fore and midships, while aft the combined cellars of the Squire and Mr Argent kept the higher orders happy. And there was the barrel of apples broached in the waist for anyone to help himself that had a fancy.

In quiet times there were exhibition bouts on the maindeck between Jem and Daniel. Ned Barker and Joby the gardener from the Hall gave displays of catch as catch can. The blackamoors and the sailors danced to the mate's fiddle and the flute which old Stilton-Wilton fished out of his papers. There were shanties and hymns led by Ben Gunn who was only forbidden to give his famous imitation of Cap'n Flint (the pirate, not the parrot). I joined in the singing but had to go easy for my voice was breaking and soared up and down the scale, now like a seagull, now like a duck, but never, alas like a nightingale.

The Inventor was busy with his latest project, the propulsion of sea vessels by steam power. But he found time to make us a device for the galley to keep pans steady when the sea rolled. Its only defect was that in calm weather it tipped 'em over and sent the porridge into the fire. But nothing could daunt old Wensleydale. As he often said to me, or to any one who would listen: "The application of reason will solve all problems." Having had "reason" across my back from a rope's end, I had my doubts, but finally concluded he was right, if all else stood still at the same time.

Wilton paced the deck, pen behind ear, paper in hand, working out shares, according to Prize Law, Treasure Trove, forms of partnership, any thing you could name. Everything was to be put into the legal pot for we had all sorts on the ship.

Mr Argent was in his element, handing Lady Alice round the deck, filling her ears with tales of the sea, all of them truer than she ever imagined. Some of them were shocking to my ears, making the Newgate Calendar read like *Miss Susan's Sampler*, but no blush bespread the creamy pallor of her cheek, as Master Hawkins might write in his epic romance. But she laughed a great deal, slapped Mr A. on the wrist and turned the said Master Jim green with one emotion or another.

Dr Livesey, when not seeing to our innards would find himself a quiet place in the sun and read in a new book he had by a Swede who claimed, so said the Doctor, that every living thing, whether it crawled, walked, flew, bit, buzzed, roared or stung could be lined up by company and column each one to its own sort and then marshalled by wider likeness into regiments and armies.

"When we get there," said the Doctor, "I shall not seek silver, for that is commonplace stuff, well on a table or round a lady's neck, but much of a muchness anywhere. I shall seek plants and creatures for my collection."

"Right you are, Doctor," I said, "when you want to go a bit of exploring, you just ask Tom and he'll put you up a snack to take along."

Jim Hawkins, who happened to pass by at the moment

looked at me strangely on hearing these words, but said nothing. Finding that Mr Argent had run off his duck, as the vulgar say, he busied himself in helping the Doctor at his work and I often saw them talking together over the Doctor's book.

I was busy at books, too. For Betsy came to me when we were fairly at sea and asked if I'd help her learn to read. Being well versed in this art I was only too glad.

And if the dog-eared copy of the manual of navigation she brought along was not as exciting as the Newgate Calendar, she seemed all the keener to read it. I was keen enough. We found a snug place in the lee of the long boat and there, arms around one another we would pore over the lines and spell out the words. One drowsy day, with the sails flapping lazily overhead and the sun warm on us, I found myself cheek to cheek with Betsy's chestnut brown face, her curly hair tickling my cheeks. Who can blame me if it awoke fond memories of Little Tilly and the cuddling and guddling on the back stairs at home? I looked at Betsy's snub nose and down at the lissom length of her and suddenly recalled the Squire's words: "After all this you might have her to wife ... we shan't ask her ..." The thought, "She's yours, Tom," flitted through my skull as I took her cheek in my palm and tilted back her head the better to kiss her.

Next moment she had thrown me on my back and straddled my waist, squeezing the breath out of me. She bent down and bit the end of my nose. It was no love bite either. She said very slow and plain,

"I say – when the kissing starts – and when the kissing – stops." Then she let me up and grinned. And said: "Tell you what, Tom. Fight you, best of three throws, for a kiss."

I glared at her and marched off while her laughter followed me round the ship. We did no reading after that, but I went to ask Ned Barker to teach me wrestling and passed the time learning the cross-buttock rather than cross-bearings. While we trained he would ask me sly, off-hand little questions, the drift of which became clear to me only later. I saw him once or twice talk to Daniel with Joby interpreting his words, and thought it strange, for generally the colliers and Squire's blackamoors kept apart.

Yes, it was strange and there were other queer things to be heard and seen by one who earns a wage (whoever was paying it) for keeping his eyes and ears open.

All around excitement was growing as we drew near to the end of our voyage. We were due to call at the island, drop a landing party and then head for Kingston, Jamaica, which lay some hundreds of miles north-east of our course, to land the crew members who were paid off, before making all speed back to Treasure Island. Everyone was in high spirits because we were so near the end of the first part of our venture.

The day came when Captain Gray let it be known that we were but a few miles from the island and would drop anchor there with first light. I worked in the galley with Molly Brindle until after sundown making ready provisions for our landing party. At last near midnight, Molly bid me good night and I was left alone.

I lingered on deck, straining my eyes through the darkness, hoping for a sight of some darker shape that might show where the island lay. But I could see nothing.

There was nought to do but go and sleep, though I felt too excited for that. As I made my way below I passed near the apple barrel and as I did heard the muffled voices of two older men talking. Before I had heard a dozen words I was listening in an extreme of fear and curiosity. The better to hear them I got bodily into the barrel and sat there in the dark, listening through a knot hole. As I did, I understood that the lives of all the honest folk aboard depended on me alone.

— 24 —

The Mutineers

"Well, John?"

"Aye, John."

"We can't go on meeting like this, the men'll suspect monkey business."

"That's what we're about. Treasure's monkey business if ever there was. What's the word?"

"The word's this. My men, Daniel, Joby and the others have come to me and made demands."

"Have they, by the mark?"

"They have. They'll raise the silver, they say, but only if they are given their freedom and paid at the going rate for their labour. I'll lay Ned Barker put 'em up to it. You should never have brought him."

"Rot me, John, Ned Barker's the bad apple in the barrel."

"So he is, and speaking of apples, John, let's step up and get an apple to wet the pipe."

You may fancy the terror I was in. I should have leaped out and run for it if I had found the strength, but my limbs and heart alike misgave me.

"Oh stow that, don't you go a-sucking that bilge. We'll have a glass or two of Bristol milk before we go to bed. Ned Barker came to me today. Said identical to what your men said. Release us colliers from the seven-year bond and pay the going rate or no silver."

"What'll we do, John – deal with 'em?"

"Your head ain't much account, John, nor ever was. If I had my way, I'd have 'em raise the treasure and stow it and

133

work us back to Kingston before I struck. We're quarter-deck men. We can't dig out and load silver. But I'm for finishing with 'em at the island, as soon as the blunt's aboard."

"But they won't load it."

"Aye, that's what we gentlemen split on – no load, no pay."

"I've a plan."

"Then, spit it out, John."

"When we heave to in Kingston, we go ashore, you and I, for you know the port, having made your way there."

"And then?"

"Why, then we buy half a dozen fresh blackamoors there and ship 'em over to Treasure Island to raise the bar silver. Once the silver's lifted, Ned Barker, Daniel and the others can take their pick, go on shore as maroons and stay there, or come home with us and be transported or sold."

"I admire you for that, John, and here's my hand on it. But not a soul must hear of it."

"Agreed, John. So, this very night, we change course and head straight for Kingston. Cap'n Gray can be trusted to keep his mouth shut. The sooner we berth there the sooner we get back with fresh hands, the better."

"Aye. One thing more, though, John. I shan't come ashore with you. Kingston's an inconvenient port for me to set foot in just now."

"Oho, what have you been up to there, John?"

"Never you mind, shipmate, Mum's the word. See here, you take Betsy with you. She'll see you right. She knows the port and the folk."

"You're mighty free with my servant, John. I reckon you know that young lady better than I do myself."

"Well, John, since we're squaring with one another, I'll tell you. Betsy served in my house in Kingston for a year before I sent her over to Bristol."

"So, you and Blandly, the rogue . . ."

"No use crying over spilt milk, John. We're in this together now, sink or swim. Who can we trust?"

"Ah, that's a question. I take it hard that Daniel turned against me. I thought better of him. Doctor and Jim Hawkins should be steady at push of pike."

"How about little Tom? Is he square?"

"Aye. He'll do ought for silver."

"You should know, you've been greasing his palm with a shilling a month."

"That I never, 'twas you who did that."

"Not I, someone's playing us double, John."

"Aye, but who? I do remember, John – funny how things go, ain't it? How I sat by this very apple barrel, making my plans with the other gentlemen of fortune and all the while Jim Hawkins was a-crouching inside, hearing every word."

"John, d'you reckon there could be someone a-spying on us now?"

In my terror at discovery I tried to clamber up and escape from the barrel. But the scraping noise of my feet against the side was heard.

The two men leaped up. I felt the barrel seized top and bottom, lifted in the air, borne along several paces then pitched clean into the sea. Too shocked and buffeted to cry out, I clung to the sides for dear life as my frail craft was lifted on the waves.

Above me the *Hispaniola* sailed on into the darkness.

— 25 —

The Mysterious Wreck

The barrel, as I had ample reason to know before I was done with her, was a very safe vessel for a person of my height and weight, both buoyant and clever in a seaway, but she was the most cross-grained lop-sided craft to manage. Do as you please she always made more leeway than anything else and turning round and round was the manoeuvre she was best at. In the end I was obliged to let the craft go her own way. The night was dark overhead, the sea immense below, but land, I guessed, was not so far away. I could see little and do nothing. So I curled up as best I could and tried to sleep.

Before I drifted off, the events of past weeks ran through my head like a Punch and Judy show, folk popping up and down like puppets, pushing to the front and being pushed back in their turn. What would Trelawney and Argent do now they'd thrown in together? What would happen to my other friends? Why was Mr Argent scared to land in Kingston? Being afraid was not his style, but plainly there was something or someone in that port who put the wind up him. That must be a creature of a very special sort. What would Squire do with his share of the silver? Furnish Lady Alice with another useless husband, or drown himself in crusty port? Would Master Jim never be cured of his two ills, writing in the grand manner and love for Lady Alice? And Betsy, lovely brown termagant Betsy, spying on all and sundry, who was she? What was she up to? How would all this plotting and manoeuvring end? One thing was sure,

I'd never get that kiss, even for the best of three throws.

I slept at last and dreamed of Old Oakleigh the undertaker, the one fixed point in all my turning twisting life. I'd learned his lesson well. Life was a game with good or bad cards. Was the end of the game near for me? A sea burial was honourable, I thought, in my dreams. I had my coffin ready made, though without a lid. But never a farewell kiss.

I woke, the sky blue over me, the sea running strong but level underneath.

Through the knot hole which was near my head, I spied at some little distance on the skyline two low hills, perhaps half a mile apart and south-west of them a third and higher hill.

It was Treasure Island.

In a second, gloom gave way to excitement. Springing up without thought, I overturned my vessel and found myself in the water. Up I struggled. All that philosophy about life's game ending and clearing the cards from the table was forgotten. Loud and clear I demanded another hand and with a kind of lurching, clawing leap I mounted astride the barrel, riding it like a fat timber horse. Ahead of me the low coastline between the two hills opened up to show an inlet with trees by the shore, or perhaps the mouth of a river. Left to herself the barrel seemed inclined to drift south across the mouth of the inlet to where I could see waves breaking over the rocks. I'd seen enough of greater vessels than mine break up under the cliffs at Black Hill cove to want to go in that direction. So using my heels as if the barrel were a horse I urged her on in the line I wanted her to take.

For a while it was nip and tuck who was master. But after an hour's paddling she came clear of the cross current and I began to edge her towards the low shore on the south of the inlet. The space between the heads was long and narrow and the woods lined the beaches on either side. Right before me, deep in the inlet, I saw the wreck of a ship. It had been a great vessel of three masts, but had lain so long exposed to the weather that it was hung about with great webs of seaweed. On the deck of it, shore bushes had taken root and now flourished thick with flowers. It was a sad sight but it showed me the anchorage was calm.

After another half hour I kicked my way to shore and sprang off into the shallows, bidding my barrel boat good-bye. Drawn as much by curiosity as ought else, I now made my way along the sandy shore down which reedy grass had crept to come closer to the wreck, festooned in its strange covering of flowers and bushes.

But there was stranger still to see. As I came near the wreck, and she was stuck hard and fast in a sandy bank, I saw that the leaves and branches aboard her had a familiar look. Not that I knew what kind of shrub they might be, but they were all of them regular in height and shape, as though someone had clipped them like a hedge. With the deck house under its canopy of moss rising above, it had all the look of a settler's cabin, surrounded by its garden.

Stranger still. From shore to ship stretched a double gang plank with a rough hand rail to give support. In a twinkling I was on it and climbing to the deck garden, as I now saw it to be. Once over the side, I saw that all around me were grass plots and flower beds, separated by neat paths through which the deck timbers, roughly patched here and there, showed through.

On one patch of grass grazed a tethered animal, a she-goat with bulging udders. Milk, I thought. I looked around me and lo and behold, hanging on a peg by the deck house door was a bucket, and beneath it a crude three legged stool. But as I approached the goat, intent on breaking my fast, it put itself on guard and set up a rapid bleating almost as if it had forgot its true nature and thought itself a watch dog.

Baulked in this, I turned to the deck house door. It was open. "Hello, any one there?" I cried. From the trees on shore came a chorus of bird noises, but no answer nearer than that of the she-goat's bleating.

Wishing I'd a hat to take off, I pushed my way inside the narrow doorway. The inside was gloomy but light enough to make out the panelled walls of a state room, with a table and four chairs in the centre. All was neat and clean and it was laid for three. But there was more, and stranger. For if my eyes did not deceive me it was laid with silver plate such as I'd seen in the best homes around Bridgwater, or at Trelawney Hall.

I stood stock still. Sunk so low in the chairs that I had not noticed them were two figures.

I guessed they were fast asleep with their hats tilted over their eyes. I stepped closer but quietly, for folk woken too suddenly can be unfriendly. On the back of each chair something was neatly carved. One read "Tom Morgan, his place," the other "Ben Creech, his place." Quieter still, I crept round and bent to look at the chairs on the other side. One was marked "Dick Johnson, his place," the other had no name on it.

I leaned on the back of the fourth chair and looked up to speak to Messrs Morgan and Creech, softly so as not to wake 'em too suddenly.

There was no point. They were not going to wake for me nor anyone else. Their eyes were sightless holes, their faces grinning skulls and their hands, stretching from the patched sleeves of their coats, bare bones.

— 26 —

A Skeleton Crew

I turned to run from that Devil's dining-room and got as far as the door. Then I saw the harmless, bleating goat with her swollen udders and stopped. Skeletons can't do harm. Ghosts don't keep goats. And whoever Dick Johnson, missing one of the trio might be, he was alive. And a neat, civilized cove, too, by all appearances, though a touch strange in the head, keeping his own mates in their bones at table with him, places laid and all.

Dick Johnson, Tom Morgan, those names rang a bell in my noddle. In Master Jim's story, three men were marooned on Treasure Island, when the whole murderous treasure hunt was done. Dick Johnson was one of them, I was sure, and there was something special about that name. He'd done something particular, he had, though I was blowed if I could recall what it was. And whatever the others had done didn't matter a tinker's cuss for they were nought but a bag of bones right now.

But, who'd turned 'em to bone? Was it Mother Nature's handiwork, or was it "Drink and the Devil" as they say in the song? Had someone helped Nature along? If so, that might be friend Dick. But if he'd done 'em in, wouldn't he hide them away, bury the corpses?

I wasn't inclined to stay and find out, so I headed for the gang plank. When something stopped me. Down in the greenery someone was singing. A voice worse than mine, but the words were familiar. I remembered them well from my workshop days.

"All people that on earth do dwell."

But he got no further than that, this singer. The next line was just noises, rum de dum and so on through the verse. Then he'd start again, with "All people that . . ." and so forth.

The sound came closer. The singing stopped, then came a voice moaning like a parson's,

"Oh Lord, open Thou our lips."

And an answering voice, more natural,

"And our mouths shall show forth thy praise.

"Oh Lord la la da da da.

"Oh Lord la da da da da," and so it went on, coming closer and closer. Then, with a "Let us pray," the bushes near the gang plank were pushed apart and out came a man, tall and skinny, leading a billy-goat by a leash like a dog. He was burnt so dark by the sun he might have passed for a blackamoor, but his long thin nose looked more like a white man's. He was dressed in goatskin breeches and jacket, and his chest was bare, burnt as brown as his face. His hair was long, and so was his beard, but they had been trimmed and kept neat. Like his home he was ship-shape in a queer way. I started to lose my fears.

Clearing my throat, I gave him the time of day. Looking up, he saw me, but waving his hand, answered:

"See you after service, young man."

With that, he marched off along the shore with the words of the Lord's Prayer rising up behind him. He vanished among the bushes and I began to think I should maybe sneak away, when he reappeared. This time he was singing again as he vanished in the woods at the stern end of the ship. When he came back, he'd started on a sermon. I heard him laying into the congregation as he went past for the fifth time, about the idle poor and the burden on the parish. It was a sermon I'd heard many a time at home and suddenly all was clear in my mind.

Dick Johnson was going back to his younger days, when he was a boy, before ever he was a sailor and a pirate. He must think it was Sunday. I thought a moment. Blow me down if he wasn't right. It was Sunday. By all that was marvellous, it was Sunday, and Dick Johnson, on this island for fifteen blessed years, knew it was.

"Now, young man, what can I do for you?"

There he was coming up the gang plank with his goat.

"You're Dick Johnson, are you?" I asked.

He stopped on the plank a foot away from me.

It was as if his memories had gone from his head. He unslung the musket that was strapped to his back and said:

"Who in thunder are you?"

"My name's Tom Carter. I'm a castaway and I mean you no harm." I held up my hands to show they were empty and backed away on to the deck. He followed me, and then stopped again and began to touch me, here and there on the chest and face.

"Are you real, Tom Carter?"

"As real as you, Dick Johnson."

"How do you know my name?"

"It's writ on the back of the empty chair."

"Aye, Dick Johnson's my name. I've to go to church alone these days. Tom and Ben, they're backsliders. Religion's no meaning for 'em."

He stared closely at me.

"Are you a Christian soul?"

I nodded and he went on eagerly,

"Then happen you know what Revelation 22, Verse 12 says?"

I shook my head. Dick sighed.

"Here's a man knows every verse in the blessed Bible, but that one."

"Why so?"

He seemed not to hear me, but went into the deck house.

"Now then, Tom, now then, Ben, you missed a powerful good sermon this day."

To my astonishment, I heard a gruff old man's voice answer. "Ah, Dick, stow that gab, you know Ben and I don't hold with all that churchifying."

"So much the worse for you. If you had gone to church as you should, you'd not be as you are now."

"Maybe you're right, Dick. What's for dinner?"

"Cold meat, sweet potatoes, pineapple to follow."

"And a touch of grog?" This came in a lighter, younger voice.

"Ah well, seeing we've a guest, we'll have a noggin." He called through the doorway,

"Come in, Tom, meet your namesake Tom Morgan, and Ben Creech."

I went in again and found him busy putting food he took from a cupboard, on to the table. I was hungry and sat down quickly. The food was good, well prepared, and when he'd said grace, mercifully short, we both set to.

"I don't cook Sundays, keeps me from going to church. Eat up now, Ben," he urged the skeleton opposite. "See how young Tom packs his grub away."

"Ah, my appetite's gone," came the answer. I shot a look at Dick. His lips were half closed and his throat muscles played up and down. He was throwing his voice like a performer in a side show at the fair.

"They don't say much, these days," he observed, as he went back to the cupboard and brought out a pitcher and a rough carved wooden cup. He poured me out a drink. It was strong and fruity. He must have had plenty of time to perfect his home brew in fifteen years. He sat down and saluted his messmates with his cup. They regarded him in silence.

"They used to be great talkers, Tom. Great argufiers too. Why, often on a Sunday evening, I've taken a text from the Good Book and we've debated it."

He drank and thought for a moment.

"One evening, I remember it well, it was five years since, we sat and discussed the meaning of the text 'Unto him that hath shall it be given and from him that hath not shall it be taken away even that that he hath.' First they debated. Then they argufied. Then they quarrelled. Finally, they came to blows. They grabbed each other by the gullet, Tom, and fought like fiends out of hell. They rolled out of the house, across the deck, over the side and into two fathoms of water on the starboard side.

"When I got to the ship's rail, they lay there on the sandy bottom, Tom, with Ben's head across old Tom's knees and the quick fish steering to and fro over both.

"I hauled 'em up. But the damage was done. Year by year, they have diminished and grown more silent, more grudging with their words."

He shook his head.

"Another noggin, Tom. I limit myself to two. Drink's a demon. Drink and the Devil have done for the rest. Drink's a demon, aye, and so is money. The root of all evil, sayeth the Book and the Book is right."

He laid his hand on mine along the table top.

"I know, Tom, lad, 'cause I'm rich, see."

— 27 —

The Black Spot

"Rich?" I said.

He looked at me more closely with those hot-coal eyes of his. I waited for his next words, my heart going like a hammer.

"Do you fancy some cheese, Tom?"

I nodded, mouth open and he rose and went to his food cupboard. He brought back a silver platter with cobs of bread and cheese in three colours. He must have dyed and flavoured them with herb and berry juice. I waited to hear more of his wealth, but he said nothing.

"Good cheese, Dick. Never tasted better."

"Aye, Tom."

Silence a moment.

"Ben Gunn were a fool."

I started.

"Ben Gunn – you wouldn't know him, Tom. He was marooned here, afore I was. What did he do?"

Ah now, thought I, we shall hear about the silver.

"He shot all the goats he could get near, drove them up to the hills. Took me the Lord's own job to wheedle 'em down again. God's creatures are worth more alive than dead, and don't you forget that, Tom. I kills one every month end, that's enough for the three of us. Tom and Ben don't eat much."

I dared not remind him of riches. How did I know what he'd say or do next?

"Aye, Ben Gunn were a fool. He found all that gold. What did he do with it?"

But Dick was not talking to me. He was looking at the other Tom.

"We know, Dick, we know," the skeleton's head answered mournfully.

"Aye, he gave it to Squire, him that marooned us here, you, Tom, and Ben there and me. Many's the time, Tom," (now he was looking at me again), "many's the time, I've sat here and vowed that if I saw Trelawney again, I'd wring his calf's head off his body with these hands."

Dick's hairy fists landed with a thump close to mine on the table. I choked on my cheese but kept still.

"I prayed that He might deliver Trelawney, like the Philistines into my hands, him or that back-stabbing Silver. But His answer is always the same. Thou shalt forgive them, Dick, forgive them seventy times seven, but thou shalt not . . ."

His voice rose to his parson's chant.

"Thou shalt not disclose unto them where the bar silver lies."

He cackled and dropped his voice.

"Because, Tom, we took it from Black Crag. Squire and the others reckoned they couldn't carry it. But we did. We dug it out and humped it over here, two hundred bars of it, and this plate, and the arms and powder. Eight months it took us, barring Sundays, that goes without saying."

"Where is it now, Dick?" I asked quietly.

He glared at me. "You what?" he roared. "Ah, you're only a boy, no older than Jim Hawkins was then, not like that swine Trelawney. Well, I'll tell you."

I squirmed in my chair.

"It's buried now, where no one can get to it. I hid it away after Tom and Ben fell out. It took me two years, as the Lord commanded. It was silver they were fighting over, intruding their heathen greed into debate over God's holy word. If it had not been for that cursed silver, they might now be hale and hearty, like you, like me, not moody and broody as they are now."

He got up and began to remove the dishes. I started to help him, but he waved me back.

"Not now. Tomorrow you shall serve at table. Then on Tuesday I shall do it. And so turn and turn about."

Oh, thought I, I hadn't planned to stay so long, not least now I knew where the bar silver was, or rather, where it wasn't, either of which was more than my shipmates knew. With fine weather, they would be back on the island in ten days or so. Dick was main hospitable, but a man who makes no difference between living flesh and bare bones made uncomfortable company. Staying with Dick would be a dodgey game, all right. Though I could see that taking leave of him might be trickier.

I discovered this that very night. We slept out on deck on the grass, under the stars. The night air was fresh and mild. Dick snored the moment he lay down. I stayed awake and when I was sure he was well away, got up very delicately. But I was barely on my feet when one of the goats bleated. Dick rose like a long shadow, presented his musket to my ear and said: "Arise, Dick Johnson, the Philistines are upon thee. Ah, 'tis you, Tom. You'll find it in the stern."

I trotted along the deck, waited a while then went back. Only when I was stretched out and breathing loud did he lie down.

Next day after breakfast he began to show me the island. He knew every blessed square inch of it, hill, forest, scrub and glen, shore line and swamp. Where the goats grazed, where the herbs and berries grew, where the birds nested, he knew all. He had small vegetable patches hidden here and there where the soil was good, like a squirrel's nut store.

"The land is good here, a host might be fed from his bounty. And there is none but me and thee."

So he thought. But not for long.

Each day we walked in a different line. South-west up the valley to the foot of Spy Glass Hill, the biggest peak in the island. South through the oak and pine woods and around the marshes, to Skeleton Island, or along the coast westwards to Haulbowline Head. He showed me where the *Hispaniola* had anchored, the tumbledown stockade where they'd fought, the remains of the camp where they'd caroused, the graves where the dead lay.

He talked to me all the time as if I knew it as well as he. And in a way I did, though how was he to know that?

But there were two places he never led me to, though I guessed where they lay. One was the cache where the doubloons had been buried, the other was the Black Crag where the bar silver had lain. It was more than cunning, though he'd his share of that. Dick was afraid of something or someone, maybe himself. Sometimes in the evenings he'd go apart in the bows and pray. I knew what the Methodies mean when they speak about "wrestling with God". His dark face would go pale grey and the sweat would stream down his hairy chest. Then he'd go limp and dull and not revive until I gave him a small cup of his own grog.

I learned to be wary on those nights for he would sprawl and cringe in nightmare, jump up and light the lamp, searching the ship from stem to stern, calling on Tom and Ben to arm themselves. One night he woke me, dragging me up by my shirt and searching my face with the lantern so that it blinded me.

"Jim Hawkins, what are you after? Tom Morgan was right, we should have done for you."

I fended him off. "Dick, it's only little Tommy Carter."

I understood that my coming had set him off. Poor old cove, he'd lived in peace with his early memories. I'd brought the later, uglier ones back to him.

But I didn't know the half of it.

Next Sunday at service I recalled two whole verses of

"All people that on earth do dwell." It was a grand occasion. At supper he was in a high old mood and Tom Morgan and Ben Creech caught it from him. They joked and told yarns some of which shocked Dick and he spoke to them sternly.

And in the small hours he woke me with his hand on my neck. Tears streamed down his face.

"Tom. You remembered the hymn. You're a Christian. Remember Revelation 22 verse 12. I beseech you."

I struggled to my feet.

"Dick, what's the fuss over a verse? You know the Bible from end to end."

He fumbled in the old bag he carried on his shoulder and fished out his dog-eared Bible, its covers tied up with cord.

"See Tom, what verse 19 says: 'And if any man shall take away from the words of the book of this prophecy, God shall take away his part out of the book of life and out of the holy city, and from the things which are written in this book.' That's clear enough, ain't it?"

"I reckon so."

"Well, see what happened to verse 12." He fumbled with the old book and the back fell off. A ragged hole the size of a coin had been cut in the final page.

"I did that, Tom. Of all the mortal things I've done in my life, He has forgiven me every one but that. 'Twas to spite Silver it was done. 'Twas to give him a warning Black Spot. But it don't make a difference to Him. Till you put back that paper as it was, Dick Johnson, He says, no paradise for you. I begged Him would it do if I found out what verse 12 says and wrote it in, and he says, well that's good, but only half good enough."

The tears flowed again.

"The Black Spot, Tom. I cut it out. I can't put it back."

28

The Stockade

The Black Spot. I went hot and cold. That hole in Dick's Bible. That little curl of paper which had dropped from Master Jim's papers that day in Merchants' Hall. Both belonged together. And Tom Carter had that identical scrap in his fob pocket along with his precious monthly shillings. One move by me and Dick Johnson's ticket to Heaven was guaranteed.

But what about mine? Supposing he found out who I was, where I was from, that I was Jim Hawkins' lad, shipped as cook with Squire Trelawney, friend of Argent or Long John Silver (or had been until he heaved me overboard)? What would Dick do? I looked at those hairy old paws pressed to his face with the tears running over them and thought what they'd do to my tender neck if they got a grip on it in anger. He'd have Trelawney's head off his shoulders. What about mine? Child's play.

Silence is golden, thought I and kept my gob shut. At last he went back to sleep and in the morning I made him an omelette with gannets' eggs we gathered off the cliff face. He was his old self again, whatever that was, and the icy lump in my guts melted away. That Black Spot paper could stay in my pocket even if Dick had to take his chance on the Pearly Gates.

I tried to put it out of my mind and think of other pressing business, not least what to do when the *Hispaniola* returned. But how could I give old Dick the slip without doing any harm, to him or me? As it happened, both matters sorted themselves out at once.

Next Saturday, Dick decided we'd go up the river. There was something on his mind that morning and he pressed on in front of me, taking great leaps over rocks or through bushes, like a goat. We followed the river up into the hills until it vanished from sight in the scrub. Still he kept on till from the top of one hillock, as we came clear of the trees, I could see, not half a mile away, Black Crag.

"There it is, Tom, where the bar silver lay. We humped it all the way to North Inlet, then I humped it to . . ." he stopped short. "Mum's the word, Tom. Not a single blessed one of 'em could stow their gab. Even Cap'n Flint himself had to make maps and signs and crosses for others to see. But not Dick Johnson.

"Ah, Flint, that were a murdering, wicked old Devil. Dear heart and he died bad for it, did Flint. How he raged and hollered for rum when the fever got him. And he sang too."

Dick stopped and his hot eyes were half closed and cunning. He put on a high trembling voice that echoed through the hot air, making the birds rise up and cry.

"Fifteen men on the dead man's chest,
Yo ho ho and a bottle of rum."

He sang.

"That were his only song and I tell you true, Tom, I never myself liked it since. It was mortal hot, like today and the windy was open and I heard that old song coming out as clear as clear."

Dick wiped the sweat off his forehead and sat down on a tree stump. "Aye, Tom, Drink and the Devil, they took him in the end. He hollered for rum, with the death haul on him."

"'Darby McGraw,' he wailed, 'Darby McGraw, fetch aft the rum, Darby.'"

The sound of Dick's voice was so fearful in these lonesome woods and his face so strange and great with the sweat on it that I cried:

"Stop it, Dick, stop it."

When he showed no signs of hearing, I had an idea. I struck up as loud as I could with:

> "All people that on earth do dwell
> Sing to the Lord with cheerful voice . . ."

On the third line he joined in and we sang it as if we'd save our lives. We sang the two verses I knew three times over.

It stopped that terrible talk of death and fever, but it threw Dick into another fit. He fell on his knees and scrabbled in his bag. Plucking out his Bible, he snatched at the cord and held it up, the mangled page uppermost.

"Oh Lord, if I might have that scrap of holy paper now, I would give the treasure to that man who put it in my hand. That would be right?" he demanded of the sky. His arms went up and he began to chant a fearful prayer pleading and begging until the woods echoed with it. I clapped both hands over my ears, but he went on. "All the bar silver every blessed ounce for that one scrap of paper."

"Dick! Dick!" I yelled. "It's here! It's here, man." I pulled open my breeches fob and jerked out the yellowed paper circle, scattering my spying shillings over the ground. By main force I hauled the Bible out of his grasp and slapped the circle into place under his very eyes.

"See, Dick, it's whole. See what it says, verse 12."

But blowed if he could see a thing. I had to read it for him.

" 'And, behold, I come quickly; and my reward is with me, to give every man according as his work shall be.' "

He snatched the Bible and clasped it to him. Then he

beckoned me to him and whispered in my ear. Then he stood up.

"Angels of heaven," he called, "now can thy servant enter in." He rose, clapped the Bible back into his bag and began to caper like one of his goats, a mad dance from rock to rock, until I thought he'd hurl himself into a ravine and beat his brains out. Without a look at me, he raced away, not into the valley towards the inlet, but away south-east towards the live oak forests, tossing off "hallelujahs" and "praise be's" as he ran.

I raced after him but, spry as I was, I had no hope of keeping up with him. He sprang over gullies, leaped logs, coursed like a hare round bushes and plunged through streamlets, sending up spray as he howled his happiness to high heaven. Not once did he look back or heed my shouts.

So hard did I follow after him that I was through a bush screen and into a slough beneath dank trailing branches before I could stop. As I strove might and main to draw myself clear I could hear him calling, his voice going deeper into the bushes and sounding fainter as he went. When I'd finally pulled myself clear and found a way round the marshy levels, there was neither sight nor sound of him any more. The woods and swamps were silent and I was on my own.

I could think of nothing better to do than make my way back to the ship in the inlet in the hope that I might find Dick had homed there. But another part of my mind told me that Dick was not on his way back to the ship, but finding the shortest route to the home he'd longed for, and whose door now opened wide for him. His crazed brain was leading his body like a Jack o'lantern deeper into the marshes where he'd be swallowed up, shouting his last "Glory be." He must be crazed, for if I'd heard him right he'd whispered that the silver was back "safe" at Black Crag.

I knew at the old ship, there'd be food, and I could wait till I had signs of the *Hispaniola* coming back. I turned in my tracks to make my way north-east so I thought, but the trees hid the sun and the sloughs hindered me on my way sending me round in circles. It was now noon and the sun, when I could spot it, was dead overhead and little guide to me. Its heat beat down heavily enough through the leaves and drew up foul vapours from the bogs around me. It came to me that I must wait until the sun dipped somewhat to give me a notion of east and west. I might then strike out for the coast and find my way north to the inlet from there. Putting my back against the nearest tree trunk and pulling up the neck of my shirt to keep insects from my face, I settled down to wait. In a while I slept.

I woke after an hour with a great noise in my ear. Was it a dream? A moment later, though, it came again, the heavy boom of a cannon on my right, It could only be the long nine of the *Hispaniola*. But what were they firing at?

Fixing the position as best I could, part by the cannon sound, part by the sun, I set out again, skirting the swamp holes and jumping from one mossy stone to another, over lush green grass, ducking under trees and pressing through bushes. Another shot from the cannon corrected my line of march. The undergrowth thinned out and I pressed on more boldly.

With a crash, a round shot ploughed through the trees not a dozen yards from me. I came out into open country to see, not a quarter of a mile away, the overgrown walls of the stockade and beheld the red flag of defiance fluttering in the air above it.

PART

— 4 —

My Shore Adventure

29

Mr Argent Surprised

(Narrative continued by Dr Livesey – from his journal)

27 August 17— Last night, two miles off our goal, Treasure Island, a tragedy. Little Tom Carter, Jim Hawkins' apprentice, our cook and general factotum, and favourite with all, lost overboard in strange circumstances. The apple barrel gone too. Did it roll off the side of the ship while he helped himself to an apple? Yet the sea was not unduly high and the wind none too strong.

No attempt made to rescue him. Jim Hawkins discovered his absence too late. A further difficulty from our sudden change of course. Instead of putting ashore a landing party we are heading for Kingston, Jamaica, which we should reach in five days, given fair winds.

28 August 17— Spoke to Squire Trelawney today, proposing we hold a memorial service for Tom. Squire thought we should wait until "this business is done". That sounded a mite callous to me and I told him so. He looked uneasy but spoke no more on the matter. Something strange in his manner.

Talked with Somerscale the Inventor, or Wensleydale as the crew call him after poor Tom's nickname. Somerscale none too pleased over that but moved by little Tom's loss. "He could call me what he likes if he were brought back to us," said he.

Somerscale questioned me about the marshes on Treasure Island. It's his opinion the gases given off may be used for lighting and other purposes, domestic and manufacturing. All it requires, says he, is "the application of reason". Plus, I should think, the application of the value of a good deal of the bar silver, if and when we raise it.

29 August 17— Still no word from the Squire why we changed course. But Mr Argent not opposed to it. If I were a cynic, which I hope never to be, I'd say the two of them are up to something. They are so affable to one another. Can it be some move to counter discontent among the servants and the colliers?

They, too, seem thick as thieves. A feeling in my bones that this voyage may prove as dangerous as the last. Pray Heaven it may not be so. Ned Barker has approached me confidentially while I treated one of his colliers for a skin ailment. Would I act as broker between them and Mr Argent and perhaps 'twixt Squire and his servants?

They seek freedom from bond and wages for their work. A large demand yet one that might be talked over. Somerscale agrees. Free labour, says he, works harder than bond or slave. He's a practical as well as a "reasonable" man.

30 August 17— Both Squire Trelawney and Mr Argent turned me down flat when I spoke to them re Ned Barker and the colliers. Squire was sullen, Argent arrogant. The two of them spend a good deal of time talking in corners. They're closer together than ever. Argent compounds it all by courting Lady Alice shamelessly. I fear she responds with an equal lack of decorum. One may picture the effect on poor Jim, whose nose is properly out of joint. Doing my best to distract him by taking him on my rounds, talking to him of science and medicine along with Somerscale. Strange to say, he's little taste for Somerscale's line of talk. Yet he and Wilton the lawyer get on like a house on fire, arguing about constitutions, habeas corpus, the case of Rex v Wilkes, etc. Takes all sorts to make a world.

31 August 17— Landfall Jamaica and later today we

docked in Kingston harbour. Bustling place, noisy, all in a hurry but in good humour, particularly the blacks who must outnumber white planters and governor's men, many times. Talk of renewed war between troops and Cimaroons or escaped slave warriors in the interior. Strange that this word "maroon" is the same as our word for abandoning a man on a lonely coast.

1 September 17— Crew, save for two men needed to work the ship back to the island, paid off, double money. Off on the town with a warning from Captain Gray to watch out for Press Gangers. Ship of the line in port looking for crew. Abominable business the Press. A sailor above all ought to be free to serve his King.

Mr Trelawney has gone on shore with Betsy as guide. It seems he is to buy half a dozen fresh blackamoors. Clearly he intends to use them to raise the bar silver and in this way outflank Ned Barker and his mates. Risky business. Hope Trelawney knows what he's at. Argent-Silver stayed on board! Why? Thought Kingston was his home port.

2 September 17— Squire back on board with Betsy, both in high spirits. All on board, myself included, amazed to see embark six blackamoors, but all women, young, middle aged, all shapes and sizes, all cheerful. At least one of them, plain for all to see, is with child. But she's as spry as the others.

Squire tells me that the women are to raise the bar silver. I raised my eyebrows at this, but Trelawney snorted and said: "Nonsense, they're as strong as horses and twice as willing as the men to do a hand's turn."

Squire doubly pleased. Says he's made a bargain. All the women recruited for the whole voyage, on payment to a certain "Nanny" of thirty guineas which is, he reckons, a fifth part of the purchase price. "Nanny" believed to be among the six, but which is she, can't say. All negotiations done via Betsy.

3 September 17— Sailed at dawn. The women are quartered on deck where they declare themselves happy. Ned Barker looks very down. He suspects rightly he has been tricked. Others on board only too content. Women wait on us hand and foot and bear a hand with working the ship.

4 September 17— Curiouser and curiouser. Silver refuses to mess with us and stays in his quarters. Has not been seen on deck since we left. Takes meals in his cabin. Looks poorly. I offered to physick him, bleed him if need be, but that makes matters worse. Leave well alone's good medicine.

5 September 17— Our ship's company increased by one. Jim H. helped me attend the birth of a babe to one of the women. No trouble. I suspect "Nanny" had seen to all before we got there. Jim eager to learn all I can teach him. Suspect our services will be needed again before we see Bristol once more.

Molly Brindle grows plump, and not from over-eating, though she works in the galley. Who's the father? That'd be asking, which I shall not.

Silver in great distress. Showed me red stained feather found in his porridge bowl. Declares it's blood. I told him rubbish, it was cochineal, a grisly practical joke. But he's right – it is blood.

6 September 17— Lady Alice piqued at Silver's neglect of her. She now seeks Jim's company. But Master Jim politely ignores her. Sauce for the goose? Lady Alice much put out. I think she tried to attend to Silver but he positively rebuffed her. No end to mysteries.

7 September 17— Only miles from Treasure Island now, Abraham Gray tells me. Ben Gunn more excited than any, which is a great deal. He intends to spend time hunting goats – with musket – though he boasts he can do it with equal ease with bow and arrow.

Ned Barker cheerful again. Says he'll be glad to walk on dry land. I doubt Squire and his master will let him off the ship. He must know this. Still a strange exuberance about the man. Has he a card up his sleeve? Ship full of peculiar goings on.

Tonight, grand concert on deck, exhibition bouts, music, slave songs and dances, colourful and lively. Lady Alice danced all the time with Somerscale. Responding to reason? Landfall tomorrow, says Cap'n Gray.

—— 30 ——

Arms and Powder

(Narrative continued by Dr Livesey)

Before dawn we approached the Skeleton Island anchorage slowly and with care. Gray is an excellent master and Silver knows the channel well, but fifteen years change a good deal. Silver came on deck with utmost reluctance, though.

Squire Trelawney called a secret conference in his cabin. Present were Captain Gray, Josh Hall first mate, and Henry King seaman, of the crew; of our party, Lady Alice, Jim Hawkins, Ben Gunn, Betsy and myself; of the Argent party, Mr Somerscale and Mr Wilton, and of course, Argent-Silver himself.

The Squire outlined a plan to secure all the colliers and blackamoors (Daniel included, though Squire very hurt to have to do this) under hatches, while our expedition lands to locate the silver cache. The women, under "Nanny", will then be landed while an armed guard is mounted over the prisoners. One musket, one pistol, one cutlass, powder and ball were to be issued to all save Lady Alice and Betsy.

Lady Alice objected strongly. "Reason indicates," said she that God created man and woman with equal spirit. Somerscale supported her. But when the matter was put to the vote it was defeated, Jim Hawkins, Wilton and myself abstaining. But I saw Somerscale pass Lady Alice something beneath the table and when she left the cabin she had a pistol tucked in her belt, her skirts hitched up and a seaman's hat on her head. Looked very fine, too. Betsy was dispatched discreetly to warn "Nanny" and the other women of the plan. All then dispersed to their posts and a guard was set on the arms and powder.

But by four-thirty o'clock it was clear that the biter had been bit. We came out on deck to find the long boat in the water and headed for shore. It was well down in the water and heavy laden. On board were Ned Barker and the colliers, the Squire's servants, Daniel included, and more astounding still, the women, Betsy included.

Captain Gray commanded them to halt as they were quitting the ship without leave. Barker answered but his words were barely audible at that distance. One of the blackamoor women made matters plainer by a signal the like of which I have not seen since with His Majesty's troops at Fontenoy.

The Squire now cried out in a loud voice to the boat:

"Daniel, it's to you I'm speaking. I order you to return to your master. I know you are a good man at bottom and I dare say not one of the lot of you is as bad as he or she makes out. I have my watch in my hand. I give you thirty seconds to join me."

There was a commotion on board the long boat, some kind of struggle.

"Come, my fine fellow," said Squire. "Don't hang so long in stays."

There was a sudden scuffle and Daniel dived from the long boat and swam strongly for the ship. When he was at mid distance from boat to ship, the Captain ordered the tarpaulin off the long nine. Josh Hall the mate, being an excellent gunner, he made it ready for action while the boat was still a little way from shore. He laid her like a master and the long boat swinging broadside on to the beach offered a target like a barn door.

"Fire," called the captain.

Right then the blackamoor women backed with a great

heave that sent the long boat's stern bodily under water. The report fell in the same instant of time. Where the ball passed, none knew precisely, but it must have been over their heads. At any rate the boat sank by the stern quite gently in a few feet of water. Some of them took complete headers, coming up drenched and bubbling. But no lives had been lost. As Daniel was hauled back aboard the *Hispaniola* and reunited with his grateful master, the others were wading ashore as fast as they could, leaving the long boat with all their gear on the sandy bottom.

They vanished from sight and sound, but not before one of their number gave us a final signal of their defiance.

—— 31 ——

The Bar Silver

(Narrative continued by Dr Livesey)

Two hours later, our party, fully armed, reached the beach and advanced with some caution into the trees. On board, we had left Josh Hall the mate, Ben Gunn and Daniel, they being enough with the long nine and the smaller swivel gun, to prevent the seizure of the ship behind our backs. Though since none of the mutineers could steer or navigate, it was felt they would not attempt this.

"I'll swear," said the Squire, "that the rogues are holed up in the stockade and intend to defy us there. What do you say? Shall we storm the place?"

Silver demurred.

"Too many for that. What's more, we don't know what arms they have. What's more if we kill too many of 'em, who'll raise the bar silver?"

There was common sense in that and Captain Gray agreed. First, said he, we must secure the treasure, put a strong armed guard on it and then regain the ship and devise some means to bring the colliers and blackamoors to proper submission.

A shot of the long nine over the stockade wall should do the trick, thought the Squire. Silver nodded at this and we set out with no more delay, the two oldest of our number in the lead, the Squire with his stick, his right foot in a slipper, Silver assisting his false leg (the ball bearings now reinstated by Somerscale) with his crutch.

At the first outset heavy miry ground and a matted marish

165

vegetation greatly delayed our progress, but by little and little the hill began to steepen and become stony under foot and the woods to grow in more open order.

Silver was guiding us and I noticed that he kept Spy Glass Hill well on the left hand. I guessed that he was avoiding passage over the point where Flint had buried the gold, where the ground was strewn with old dead bones and mournful souvenirs of his last bloody attempt to seize the treasure.

It seemed to me he increased his pace, though he was setting a hot one, vying with Trelawney, until we were well past the point where the old treasure cache lay to our east, and the stockade with its ill assorted mutineers to our west.

At ten of the morning, when we had gone, by my calculation, three miles and Spy Glass Hill lay a little way behind us, Gray decreed a halt. When Silver and the Squire protested he told them drily that he did not have the men to carry them back all the way to the ship. So we made a halt on a little plateau, amid thickets of green nutmeg trees, and with the broad shadow of the pines betwixt us and the growing heat of the sun. And it was here we received the first of several shocks.

As we made to sit down on the grass and unpack our provisions, Silver uttered a cry and pointed to the ground, his face the hue of tallow. Some yard or two away lay a mess of blood-stained feathers as though a fox had but lately left his dinner.

"'Tis Nanny's work," muttered Silver.

"What?" Squire nudged him. "What's between you and Nanny? What sins are finding you out?"

But Silver clenched his teeth and would say no more. Nor would he seat himself till Gray had shifted our resting point a good hundred yards away. There we rested, ate and drank. There was a good wine to drink, which made me think of poor Tom, our only casualty so far. Jim Hawkins too was thoughtful and I rallied him over it. He sighed.

"I think of Dick Johnson and Tom Morgan and the other we marooned fifteen years ago."

"Ha," scoffed the Squire, "ghosts now. I doubt if they lasted a month with the rum and the fever."

"Reason demonstrates," remarked Somerscale, "that ghosts are a material impossibility. A thing with no substance, can have no existence."

"Would you deny the existence of God, sir?" roared the Squire.

But Somerscale was not to be bullied.

"Were the time more suited, I would gladly debate. But I think there are other matters to occupy our attention."

"You don't have to believe in ghosts," sagely remarked Henry King, "to be feared on 'em."

"It is in the nature of the superstitious mind," said Somerscale, "to be afraid of that which it does not understand."

And in that moment he dropped the meat he held in his hand and gasped.

"What was that?"

"Why, nothing, man," replied Gray, somewhat irritated by the turn in the conversation. He ordered us to pack and move on without more ado.

Somerscale's hearing was not at fault though. Some few moments later we came out of the trees into more open ground and Silver pointed triumphantly at a dark hill some mile and a half away.

"Black Hill Crag," he yelled, and went off at a cracking pace, the Squire close behind him. Both were beaded with sweat and their coats stained dark with it. But the rest of the party, young or old were hard put to keep up with them.

Then Silver came to a sliding halt, his hand in the air.

"Hsst. What was that?"

We halted. It was no use to assert we heard nothing for it was plain to all. Out of the middle of the trees to our right, a high trembling voice struck up the well remembered words:

> "Fifteen men on a dead man's chest.
> Yo ho ho and a bottle of rum."

I have never seen men so dreadfully affrighted. The colour went from all faces like enchantment. Silver grovelled on the ground.

"It's Cap'n Flint, by . . ."

Gray, his face the colour of his name, cried, "This won't do. Stand by to go about. This is a rum sport. Can't make it out, but it's someone skylarking. It's flesh and blood you may lay to that."

"Reason indicates," said Somerscale shakily, "that spirit voices cannot have echoes, yet that voice echoed most distinctly."

As if to prove the point the song rang out again, further to our left, but quite distinctly.

"Why, by the powers," yelled Silver, "'tis Ben Gunn." Others in the party nodded, but this comfort did not last.

"You fool," snapped the Squire. "We left Ben Gunn on board."

"Shiver my timbers," gasped Silver, "so we did and no mistake. Yet, mark me, shipmates, that voice is familiar. 'Tis someone known to us."

As if to help him the voice came again in a faint, distant wail, echoing among the far off peaks.

"Darby McGraw," it wailed, "Darby McGraw. Fetch aft the rum, Darby."

"That does it," said someone. "Let's go."

"Avast there," said Silver, and his voice brought terror

to the eyes of Trelawney. "That ain't Ben Gunn. That's Dick Johnson, whom you marooned here. Dick Johnson, as I live."

"But Dick's dead," said Squire, his normal colour gone. Now the whole party was rooted to the spot, for another voice was heard, younger and deeper, hard by the first.

"All people that on earth do dwell," it sang. Now both Silver and Trelawney were ashen to the lips.

"That's little Tommy Carter that we – lost overboard," they cried.

Captain Gray now proved himself a leader. Drawing up to his full height, he ordered advance at top speed and set off at such a spanking rate towards Black Crag that we were bound to follow him. Once more the mournful singing echoed behind us and to our right, and then was silence and all we heard was the scuffling of feet on stone and soil.

Now Trelawney and Silver, all terror forgotten, took the lead, vying with each other, swaying to and fro, even fending one another off when the way narrowed. Their eyes burned in their heads, their feet grew speedier and lighter, their whole soul was bound up in that fortune, that whole lifetime of extravagance and pleasure that lay waiting them at the end of the trail.

Silver on his crutch, Squire on his stick, hobbling grimly, nostrils standing out and quivering, cursing like madmen when the flies settled on their faces, pressed on until we were right at the foot of the crag.

"Huzza, mates, all together," they cried.

Suddenly, not ten yards further, we beheld them stop. A low cry arose. Silver doubled his pace, digging away with the foot of his crutch like one possessed. Next moment we had come up with them and were at a dead halt. Before us were signs of where a great excavation had been. Lying on the ground near it was a board, branded with hot iron the name of Flint's ship, *Walrus*.

But the excavation was filled, covered with rocks and boulders, heaped up ten feet high, as though from a huge landslide.

Nothing was more clear. We would never get a sight of that silver without the aid of Ned Barker and his merry men – and women.

— 32 —

Red Shift

(Narrative continued by the Doctor)

There never was such an overturn in this world. Each stood there as though they had been struck. Though I could see from Somerscale's face that he was calculating minutely the force required to remove the rocks and the likely available sources of power to bring it to bear.

But with Silver and the Squire the blow passed instantly. Flinging aside crutch and cane with oaths and cries, they began to dig with their fingers, heaving and straining at the larger rocks, hurling the smaller ones aside.

"Dig away, gents," said Jim Hawkins with the coolest insolence. "You'll find some pig nuts and I shouldn't wonder."

"Pig nuts," bellowed the Squire. "Did you hear that? I tell you now that young man hoped for this all along. Look in the face of him, you'll see it written there."

But Silver cooled down and looked at Jim in the queerest way possible.

"I take that hard from you, Jim. I've always had the highest regard for you."

Jim began to laugh, his face lighter and clearer than I'd seen it for a long time.

"Why, can't you see," he said, turning to all of us. "This is revenge on Silver. This is silver's revenge. You'll never shift those stones."

"Fiddlesticks," cried the Squire. "Get those fools in the

stockade working and we'll be at it within the week."

"Reason indicates," said Somerscale, "that human effort is a match for any obstacle."

"It also indicates," said I, putting in a word after much thought, "that we must find some way of reconciling ourselves with our labour."

With that, Gray took command once more. He observed the one bright aspect – the bar silver needed no guard.

With that observation, he ordered a quick march back to our base on the *Hispaniola*. Quick march was a touch optimistic, for our two greyhounds were now well on the leash with fatigue and this time it was Gray at the front who set the pace while Squire and Silver brought up the rear. I kept an anxious eye on both of them, as did Jim Hawkins. He said poor Tommy Carter had been our only loss so far. But at any moment I surmised, studying the purpling faces of the two rearguards, we might have one or two cases of stroke on our hands. But Somerscale's false leg did him credit and bore Silver well on the three-hour march to the beach. Equally well did his gouty leg bear the Squire and it occurred to me that perhaps a regime of exercise, coupled with abstinence from port might make a whole man of him once more. But I determined to defer proposing it until the chances of a stroke were smaller.

We reached the shore in early afternoon and were relieved to find the gigs at their place, drawn up on the beach. That seemed to me a good sign, for we had left them unguarded and the stockade party could easily have disabled them. Unless they feared to approach the shore under the watchful eye of Master Gunner Hall and his team, who now signalled us from the ship that all was well.

Back on board, we washed and refreshed ourselves and gathered in the cabin for a council of war. We were, as I feared, sharply divided between those who were for a reconciliation with Ned Barker's company for the sake of a quick return to work and those in favour of simply talking along the barrel of a cannon.

But in the end it was decided we would send a truce party under a white flag. Led by Captain Gray for authority it would contain Ben Gunn as a sign of amity and Mr Wilton as a sign of willingness to negotiate.

The terms on which the Squire and Silver insisted and which I thought unduly harsh, were that first the bar silver should be raised, then the question of freedom and payment would be favourably considered. They were to be given an hour to give us a reasonable answer and, failing that, in the words of the Squire, "so much the worse for them". He was for adding an undertaking to clap them in irons and ensure them a fair trial, but I demurred at that, and Jim Hawkins and Somerscale supported me.

Our party went ashore and came back after some little time, Captain Gray looking somewhat disgruntled. Ned Barker had remarked that our terms were reasonable in the highest degree. They were merely the wrong way round. First there should be guarantee of freedom, then half the silver might be lifted. Then talk of wages and the lifting of the rest.

"The unmitigated gall of the man," fumed the Squire, and was for starting the bombardment right away. But he was persuaded with some difficulty to wait. An hour then having passed without a sign from the mutineers, Captain Gray ordered Hall to fire a warning shot over the stockade.

The long nine boomed and the round shot curved over the top of the trees and fell into their mass with a distant thump. After a further half hour a second shot was fired, a third and a fourth, each one, in Hall's judgement, landing a little closer to the stockade. On the fourth shot, we saw a flag hoisted over the stockade.

"'Tis the flag of truce," cried the Squire.

"Nay," observed Silver, glass to his eye, "'tis the red flag of defiance."

Lady Alice took the glass from his limp hand, and levelled it.

"'Tis Betsy's red shift," she declared.

Josh Hall fired ten more shots, all in a ring around the stockade, then three which he reckoned landed within it.

But still the red flag flew.

"We must take 'em by storm," said the Squire.

"This is not a militia exercise," said Gray stiffly and I had much ado to hide a smile. "There are too many of them to do it without loss."

"Half of 'em are women," declared Squire.

"Reason indicates," began Lady Alice, but the Squire had had his belly full of reason for that day.

"Break out the explosive shot," he proposed.

Gray looked shocked.

"One such round inside the stockade might kill or maim all. 'Twould be inhuman."

"And defeat our purpose," added Somerscale. "Since the object is to compel them to work, killing them contradicts this."

The Squire stamped along the deck.

"A trifle more of that man," he observed, "and I shall explode."

But Somerscale was not finished yet.

"The application of mental powers to this problem indicates a scientific solution."

"Confound your science," retorted the Squire.

"No," said Silver, scratching his false leg thoughtfully. "Let Mr Somerscale speak."

"I have for some time," said Somerscale, ponderously, while the Squire walked away along the deck, "considered the possibility of utilizing the gas given off by the marshes. This may be, without great difficulty, collected. A projectile, sirs, which upon impact released a quantity of this vapour, would overpower the stockade party without loss of life, or with acceptable loss of life, and," he added thoughtfully, "no damage to property or equipment. It would thus embody the principles of reason and humanity in perfect proportion."

He turned to the rest of us and Lady Alice fixed her eyes on him.

"Reason indicates . . ." he began.

"Mr Inventor," said Daniel, his voice coming from a little way towards the stern.

"Reason indicates," Somerscale went on, somewhat put out at the interruption.

"Mr Inventor," said Daniel once more. "Shut your mouth."

At this piece of effrontery all eyes turned towards the blue-clad coachman, where he sat on the stern-castle roof, behind the small swivel gun, which he had turned so that the muzzle covered the main deck.

"D—n me," said the Squire, "the rogue speaks English, after all."

—— 33 ——

Daniel Speaks

(Narrative resumed by Tom Carter)

Seeing the red standard rise over the stockade made me halt in my stride. Someone was entrenched there, but who? Someone was firing from the *Hispaniola*, but who? From what I remembered of Master Jim's account, life on this island was a chancy business with folk changing sides more often than they changed their shirts.

But that wasn't a flag, thought I, and let out a yell. It was a shift, Betsy's shift. She was there, then, and I would see her soon.

Then I stopped. Because a lady's underwear flies in the wind, does that mean she's on the spot?

What was more, who was on which side, and which side was I on? I must be a born soldier, for I made my mind up in a trice. The cannon balls were coming this way. I must get out of the line of fire. I skirted the stockade and began to set course for the east coast of the island. This way I kept clear of the round shot and could avoid all chance of observation from the anchorage where I guessed the *Hispaniola* lay and whence came the round shot. It was already late in the afternoon although still sunny and warm. As I continued to thread the tall woods I could hear from far below me the continuous thunder of the surf. A few hundred paces more and I came out of the woods and saw the sea lying blue and sunny to the horizon, and the surf tumbling and tossing its foam along the beach.

I took the cover of some thick bushes and crept warily up to the ridge of the spit which guarded Skeleton Island to the west. Behind me was the sea, and in front the anchorage. The anchorage under the lee of Skeleton Island lay still and leaden. The *Hispaniola* in that unbroken mirror was exactly portrayed from the truck to the water line. Aboard I could see some eight or ten people grouped around the brass barrel of the long nine.

The firing had stopped, the smoke had cleared round the gun, and from my hiding place, by straining my eyes, I could see who was there. Squire and Mr Argent I spotted first, levelling glasses and standing like admirals with hands behind their backs. Wensleydale and Stilton, the long and short of it, were easy to make out. Dr Livesey paced the deck a little apart with Master Jim. But who was that striding to and fro in a cocked hat – could it be Lady Alice?

I measured the distance to the ship which swung gently round till her stern faced my way. I could approach from this direction without being seen. But how? Could I swim a quarter of a mile? No.

Close by me, amid the scrub on the sand spit, was a small uprooted tree, its short branches picked clean by some grazing animal. The *Hispaniola* was still stern first towards me so I stepped out of cover and gave the tree a heave. At first, it seemed set fast, but with a couple more tugs it came free and slid splashing into the water, which was a fathom deep at this point. I grasped a loose branch and tumbled astride the trunk. I'd to shove hard with my oar because the same current which swung the ship at anchor pinned me to the shore. Instead of fighting it head on, I sidled my tree boat seaward to get clear of the tow and work round to the starboard side. This meant exposing myself to anyone keeping a look-out, which I was in no mood to do. Having left the ship in a hurry the last time, I'd no notion how I might be received on board. But I was in luck for, as I paddled clear of the current and out to circle the ship's stern, I heard voices from the deck and the sound of running to and fro. There was some to do aboard which would keep any look-out occupied.

Digging away with my paddle, half crouched on my tree trunk, I was a score of paces from the side of the ship when the current took my craft, swung it round and bore it swiftly alongside and under the stern. So quickly did it happen, I'd no time to do more than grasp with my hand at the ship's timber.

My hands came across a light cord which was trailing overboard across the stern bulwark. Instantly I grasped it. I pulled in hand over hand on the cord and when I judged myself near enough, I heaved up and commanded a view of the interior of the cabin. It was empty and the table bare with chairs grouped round it, as if for a conference. One window was open and by a bit of juggling I could switch my hold from rope to window ledge, aiming to squeeze through the gap.

A sudden screech told me the cabin wasn't empty.

"Ten per cent, take it or leave it. Ten per cent . . ." Cap'n Flint, perched on a chair back, stared me in the face. How to silence her? She wasn't close enough to grasp her scraggy neck and I suspected that a bird which had served with every cut-throat from Henry Morgan onwards would put up a good fight and kick up a deal of fuss. Quick as a thought I answered.

"Seven and a half, and not a penny more."

And leaving her brooding over that offer, I got my foot on the window ledge and hoisted my whole body on the cabin roof. Had the bird given the alarm? The shouts and running to and fro had stopped. The ship was dead quiet. Flat out on the cabin roof I stared in amazement. The first I saw was Daniel. He was crouched down, back towards me, aiming the swivel gun down in the waist of the ship. Two pistols were laid on the deck at his back. But whose side was he on?

Below him, staring up in amazement were the rest of them, Mr Argent, Squire, Captain Gray to the fore. In that moment Mr Trelawney spoke as though he were coaxing a child.

"Come now, Daniel, don't be hasty, Mr Somerscale was just proposing."

"He's proposing. I'm disposing."

Blow me down, I thought. He speaks English, the sly dog. All these years of folks talking in front of him and he making out he couldn't speak a word. Now he'd started, where would he stop?

"Mr Inventor says he don't want to kill useful labour. That's very reasonable. There ain't no reason then, why I shouldn't blow you to Kingdom come."

I could see them mulling that one over, Somerscale in particular. Reason applied down the barrel of a gun has a way of fixing the attention. But Mr Argent, I noticed, had shifted to the side and was bending down fiddling with something. I could see him, but I don't think Daniel was paying attention. Maybe he was taken up with his first speech in English.

"Now, I'm going to be reasonable. First thing I'm going to do is to ask Mr Hall to fire a rocket. That's going to bring the stockade people on board. Then we're going to . . ."

But we didn't find out what Daniel was going to do, for Mr Argent with great agility, whipped off his false leg and slung it, spinning through the air. The toe caught Daniel on the forehead, and the top swivelling round on Somerscale's ball bearings, clouted him on the back of the head. Down he fell, out cold, across the breech of the gun. Mr Argent was hobbling up the companion way just as I jumped down, whipped up the pistols and leaped with one bound into the shrouds. Hooking my leg round the cordage to hold myself secure, with pistol in either hand, I addressed him.

"One step more, Mr Argent, and I'll blow your brains out. Dead men's shares don't count," I added with a chuckle.

Was he abashed? Not a bit.

"Why, Tom, lad. See here." He looked over his shoulder at Squire Trelawney. "See here, John, didn't I say that was no ghost. Little Tom's safe and sound, after all. Just come back to play a joke on us. Mind you," he said to me, "you gave us a shock when you didn't show up that morning."

I saw the Doctor looking at Squire's livid face. His brain was going eighteen to the dozen and he didn't like what he was working out.

"D—n me," said Gray. "That was you we heard singing over at Black Crag . . . and . . ." his voice trailed away, "was that Dick Johnson too?" If the Squire had any colour in his cheek it was all gone too.

"Aye, that was Dick Johnson, and . . ." I had to add, "he's almighty keen to get a sight of you, Mr Trelawney, sir, and you, Mr Argent."

When they'd chewed that one a bit, I went on. "I'll tell you something else. He and the others shifted that treasure."

That flattened 'em. Only Jim Hawkins grinned.

"Shifted?" wheezed the Squire.

"Aye, shifted it. It took 'em eight months."

I waited a little while, enjoying the consternation on their faces, then, said:

"But Dick put it back and battened it down . . ."

"He never . . ." declared Gray.

"With the help of the Lord . . ." I added.

"Where?"

"Black Crag."

"Ah," he said. "I understand," but he'd a baffled air about him.

"Where's Dick now?" quavered Squire.

"That I can't say," I answered, "but I hope he's where he wants to be along with Tom Morgan and Ben Creech."

Mr Argent's voice took on a wheedling note. "Ah, Tom, lad, all this talk of Dick Johnson a-looking for us, is just your joke, eh?"

All the while he was sidling forward till he was near the swivel gun and his hand was reaching out for that blessed leg of his. He had it in the air when I fired both barrels. One shot took his hat and wig clean off and gave him a nice new parting in his grey scrub. The other one hit the false leg amidships. It collapsed and dangled down limply.

"Oh, my ball bearings," called Wensleydale. "You young vandal."

"Stap me," swore Argent. He took the leg and flung it overboard.

"That for your marvels of science," he cried. Grasping the barrel of the swivel gun with both hands he hauled himself up.

"Now, since you've fired off both barrels, Tom, lad, you'll have no objection if I take over this swivel gun, ready for when the stockade party reaches the ship." Supporting himself on his elbow, he called out:

"Send up that signal rocket, Mr Hall."

Then he began heaving himself up again. But just when his face was level with the cannon's mouth, Daniel struggled to his feet, picked up the slow match and held it over the touch hole.

"Mr Argent, I'm going to put your head on the top of Spy Glass Hill."

"Just my little joke," said Mr Argent, and fainted clean away.

—— 34 ——

End of the Hispaniola

By sunset, the stockade party had come down to the beach, righted the long boat and rowed back to the ship. I noticed Betsy first, for she'd thrown her white gown away and wore only the shift which she'd taken from the flag pole.

The ship party was disarmed. Ned Barker and Daniel set a guard for the night, but there was really no need. The fight had gone out of the Squire and Argent. My return from a watery grave and my news of Dick Johnson had taken the heart out of them. They didn't know whether to believe me about the bar silver (to tell you the truth I didn't know whether to believe Dick Johnson or not). But if it were in the cache they couldn't shift it without coming to terms with the stockade people.

I made supper, with Molly Brindle, who told me all that had happened while I had been separated from them, including the Squire's fatal error in bringing the slave women on board. Trelawney and Argent spent their time with Wilton-Stilton working out what they should do on the morrow. Wilton began to draft a contract which looked very reasonable, on paper as they say. It met all demands and would be signed by all parties so the way would be clear to get at the treasure "wherever and in what state that may be," it read. Even old Wensleydale couldn't be more reasonable than that. He, poor chap, was busy thinking how he could dredge up that false leg and put it right. I don't think he would forgive me for that for a long time.

When the morning came, all was ready for some hard

bargaining, or so we thought. But when we all gathered on deck, there was another shock waiting.

Daniel, as cool as you like, waves aside the document offered by Mr Wilton, and says.

"We don't want any paper. We're taking the ship."

"The ship?" explodes Captain Gray.

"The ship. We're bound for Jamaica."

The Squire was disbelieving.

"They'll clap you in irons the instant you land."

"What you've done means five hundred lashes and a rope neck-tie."

"Mr Trelawney, sir, I don't need you to tell me what they do to runaway slaves. But we're not going to Kingston. We're heading for Rio Grande on the windward side where the 'Maroons are. Kingston ain't the place for us. But don't fret. We'll send 'em word, so they can come and fetch you. Always assuming they're going to believe the word of a no 'count nigger."

"You'll never navigate the ship," said Gray.

"We could take you along with us, Cap'n," said Daniel playfully.

Gray went red.

"I'll never sail under duress."

"Then you stay here. Betsy's going to navigate. She's read the manual back to front, forwards and backwards."

Mr Argent and the others began to laugh, but Daniel flapped his hand at them.

"Makes no odds what you think. We're going. You folks think we can't raise a sail and lay a course and turn that old wheel. Well, you're going to find out. I tell you what, Mr Trelawney. When Job and I were shipped over from Benin coast ten years back, the crew was so down with yellow fever, they had us up from below to man the vessel."

His voice got louder.

"They made us sail ourselves into slavery. Well, we're

sailing right out of it."

He paused a while, and looked us over, sizing us up, I thought, as if he intended to make a purchase.

"Doctor can come with us. We need him. Besides, he can hunt for flowers and flies over there as much as he likes. Step over this side, Doctor."

Squire's eyes grew big and round as the Doctor did as he was bid.

"Ned Barker can come with us, for he's a good man. He can't help the colour of his skin. It ain't our fault how we are born, but we can rise above it."

My, what a preacher Daniel would make, I thought.

"Molly Brindle can come, 'cause she and Joby have business together." Molly, plump in the belly and pink in the cheeks, stepped over.

"Little Tom can come, because he helped, and Jim Hawkins 'cause he did no harm. You others can come, except Squire, Lady Alice, Mr Argent, and the Inventor and the Lawyer, them we don't need the way we're going to live.

"Those that don't come with us, we'll set on shore. We'll share out the stores, the arms and powder, man for man and woman for woman. Then we sail. I reckon you've got a month. You can fish, swim, lie in the sun, hunt for treasure. It'll be a real holiday. That is if folks in Kingston believe us . . .

"That's about it," he finished.

There was a silence. Then Jem Morris spoke up. "I'm stepping over. I've a few bouts to go before I beat Daniel." Henry King, to Captain Gray's annoyance stepped over, too. I think he had his eye on one of the black girls.

Jim Hawkins shook his head. "I'm sorry to say farewell to you, Doctor, but I intend to get home. I never wanted this voyage, and it's come to no good. But I'll stick with our company."

Ned Barker said: "I shall stay here. As far as I am concerned, I'm in dispute with my employer and it's against trade principles to take another service while in dispute. Besides," he grinned, "there's months of steady work on that bar silver, at the going rate."

They looked at me then. I thought a while, looking at Betsy. But she avoided my look as if to say – make up your own mind.

"I'll stay with Master Hawkins. He was good to me when I needed it. I'll not desert him now. Besides I don't like long sermons."

So, it was done. The ship's company split into two parties one to stay on board, the other to go ashore. The dividing up of stores followed. The long boat was lowered once more and the shore party's goods stacked on the beach. Then the long boat came back to take us ashore. The ship party lined the deck and we passed between their ranks and climbed down the side into the boat.

Mr Somerscale, with Lady Alice on his arm, remarked to Daniel as he passed, "It seems to me your society, founded upon irrationality, setting its face against progress and the march of history, is bound to fail." To which Daniel replied with a grin.

Jim shook hands with the Doctor. Both were deeply moved. I was sorry to say goodbye to Dr Livesey, a fine gentleman.

Next went Ben Gunn, Mr Hall and little Wilton with his bundle of papers. I'm sure he'd gladly have signed on with Daniel and worked out a constitution sweet as kiss me hand.

Then it was Mr Argent's turn. As he made to leave the ship a plump black lady, with grey hair stepped in his path, arms akimbo.

I guessed this was Nanny, the leader of the slave women.

"Oh you do well to go pale, John Silver. You know that every last one of your troubles came from me. I'm plaguing you now, like you plagued me once."

She spoke to everyone. "When he went a treasure hunting I looked after his money from the Spy Glass Inn in Bristol. I was his wedded wife but with no paper to prove it. So when we met up in Kingston and he was set to become a fine rich trader I asks him when we go to church. But that didn't suit him."

She stepped forward. Mr Argent stepped back. I've never seen him so put down, his lips were shaking.

"Respectable white men in Kingston don't have dark wives, no sir. They keep them in the kitchen and the shanty down the garden. But that didn't suit me. So he never saw me from that day to this. But I've watched him.

"You thought you were smart, setting Betsy to spy on Squire. But who sent Betsy to you when she was fourteen? That was me."

My ears pricked up at that. One mystery was solved. Those monthly shillings came from Betsy.

Mr Argent gritted his teeth. "You put those feathers on my plate."

Nanny grinned sweetly. As if it were too much for him, Mr Argent turned on his heels and suddenly hobbled off down below.

"D—n me," said the Squire, stopping by the ship's rail and turning to Nanny. "Betsy, she's your daughter."

Nanny nodded. The Squire roared with laughter.

"Don't you cackle so much," she told him. "'Cause you can't go back to Kingston."

"What?" said the Squire.

"'Cause you'll be charged with removing six slave women from the custody of their masters, without permission, and some of 'em from their husbands. Your name's dirt in Kingston right now."

Eyes round, lips clapped shut, the Squire clambered down into the long boat, aided by Jim and the first mate.

When my turn came I looked for Betsy, but her face was still turned away from me. We didn't say a word. That kiss was unkissed and that was the end of it.

Then Mr Argent came, managing his crutch with his usual skill. His face had got back its colour. I wondered if he'd taken a long swig of rum while he was down below. But there was no smell about him. He looked calm, strangely so, it seemed to me, unless it was relief at getting out of Nanny's reach after all these years.

Captain Gray now came down, saluted the ship and we bent to the oars.

As we moved away from the ship, Nanny's voice sounded from above.

"You thought you were riding high, John, but you were digging a pit for yourself. Squire – he's too slow to catch fever. You're too smart for your own good. Goodbye."

Suddenly, Mr Argent grinned and turned in the stern of the long boat.

"Goodbye, Maisie Jane (the only time I heard Nanny's name uttered). Goodbye for good."

Soon the nose of the long boat ran into the sand and we were busy unloading our stores. From the water we heard the anchor rattle up and Betsy's voice giving her commands. I paused in my labour to watch the ship come about and head through the channel alongside Skeleton Island. At my side, Captain Gray nodded grudgingly as he watched. "About right, south-south-west to clear the head, then beat up on the westward side."

The sails filled with wind. She was a brave sight the old *Hispaniola* and I noticed Master Jim looking a little sadly after her.

"That's the last we'll see of the *Hispaniola*," he said.

He spoke truer than he knew. At that moment we heard Nanny's voice again as through a loud hailer.

"Now, John, one last thing to chew over. Betsy's my

daughter. Right? Well, she's yours as well. She was in my belly when you turned us out, but you never knew."

"You're lying!" shrieked Mr Argent. Back came a mocking laugh as the ship got under way past Skeleton Island.

"Look at Silver," said Master Jim, laying his hand on my arm.

For a moment Mr Argent stood as if struck by lightning. Then he groaned aloud and began to stumble and stagger, his crutch working in the soft sand, down to the headland.

"Heave to," he howled. "Heave to." But by now the *Hispaniola* was out of earshot.

Soon she would be out of sight, for the blue of the sky was paling into dusk. We could see Mr Argent at the end of the headland, outlined against the sky, his arms spread out in an attitude of supplication towards the disappearing ship. Then a hump on Haulbowline Head to the south-west took her from our view.

"Come now," said Captain Gray. "Let's get these goods under cover before dark. We'll rig up a sailcloth awning."

"Agreed," said Master Hawkins. "I'll never go near that stockade."

We were busy with our fetching and carrying when Mr Argent appeared, hobbling slowly along the shore. His clothes hung on him like a scarecrow's, his stockings were ripped and dirty. He had lost his fine, buckled shoe. His face was a picture of utter despair.

Trelawney looked at him and put down the cask he carried. He took a step towards Mr Argent.

"Silver, what is it?"

Before our astonished eyes, that gentleman began to weep. The tears ran down his sagging cheeks.

"My daughter. She was my daughter."

"Well, man. That can't be helped now. You shifted without her till now. No good blubbing about it."

"You fool," snarled Mr Argent. "You don't know . . . I've . . ."

Mr Trelawney stumbled over and seized Mr Argent by his coat.

"You villain, what have you done?"

Mr Argent spoke through clenched teeth.

"I went below . . . laid a powder train."

"You did what?"

"A powder train . . ." Mr Argent went on, his eyes rolling in his head.

"In God's name, why?"

"That she-cat . . . tormented me . . . rid myself of her for good . . ."

"Blackguard, murderer," cried the Squire, hurling Mr Argent from him and drawing his cutlass.

They fought like demons. If one of those crazy, scything swipes had found its mark they would have been split from head to gut. And I began to wish that Squire would strike home and slice that smiling villain's head from his shoulders. Now at last I understood what was in Master Hawkins' mind about this island and all that went with it.

As they rolled around each other, rapidly exhausted, Captain Gray drew his pistol. He beat with the barrel upon an iron bar. It made a ringing sound as when Old Oakleigh beat on the handfast in the workshop in the days gone by. The fighting stopped, the two old men lay sprawled in the sand.

As the sun went down, shadows crept along the beach and the sea breeze stirred the pines. There was silence.

"Let us pray," said Captain Gray and folded his hands. We fell to our knees.

"Our Father, which art in heaven . . ."

As he reached the words, "forgive us our trespasses," we heard out at sea a dull roar as Silver's powder train blew the *Hispaniola* apart.

189

—— 35 ——

Best of Three

We lay that night under the tarpaulin. I did not sleep but in a waking dream saw Betsy bend over me, but with her face turned away. Her face and shoulders glistened with water.

She stood there a while, then vanished. In the morning after I'd made breakfast, Captain Gray assembled us.

"It's clear we cannot expect rescue. Our only hope of that lies at the bottom of the sea."

Squire Trelawney protested.

"I'll wager Blandly will soon enough fit out a consort when we don't show up."

"Ha!" Mr Argent, who sat huddled up on the sand some little distance from our group, sneered. "Blandly has played both ends against the middle these fifteen years and more. If you expect rescue from those quarters, expect away."

"You hold your mouth, sir. No one wants your opinion," snapped the Squire.

"Order, order," commanded Captain Gray. "We must set our minds on what to do. To push ahead and build a boat, for to set out to sea in the long boat with our numbers would be folly. Or to build a hut for a longer stay."

"What of the treasure?" demanded Mr Trelawney, but at a look from Captain Gray he said no more.

"Let's vote on the matter," said Ned Barker.

"A vote?" asked Mr Trelawney. "What, pirate fashion?"

"No," retorted Ned, "workshop fashion."

That was agreed. But first of all, said Captain Gray,

we should divide into parties and search the shore to the west of the island. It might be that there would be survivors. Failing that, it might be that useful stores and timbers would be washed ashore.

That was done with a will. Our company split up by twos and threes. Lady Alice, Mr Somerscale and I took the furthermost reach of the shore, where Spy Glass Hill and its cliffs frowned down at the sea.

That suited my miserable mood.

We searched all morning. They searched steadily, talking quietly together the while. I ran ahead and back like a madman, till weariness forced some sense into my head. Sensible or not though, our search yielded nothing, not even a ship's plank along two miles of beach and cliff-foot. When afternoon came we heard the musket shot from the south-east that ordered us to abandon our search. We were then in a curving bay, fringed with trees and spread with silver sand, south of Spy Glass. Lady Alice and the Inventor sat down in the shade to rest. I heard their voices as I wandered down the beach and stood, feet in the waves, looking seaward.

"With rational thought . . . great things accomplished . . . this island . . . the natural bounty of the earth . . . scientific principles . . ."

I wondered if they would be voting for a ship to be built. They seemed set on an island paradise. The water flowed around my bare knees as I waded further out, soft and smooth as milk and warmed by the sun. My toes sank gently in the sand and small creatures squirmed and scurried away as I moved forward.

Was that a driftwood plank out there, where the sun's rays sparkled on the water? I stepped forward, shading my eyes but could not see. Sun, sky and waves played tricks with the sight, making strange shapes. Lack of sleep and misery weighed down my body. My eyes closed and I stepped further and deeper in.

Life was a game after all, whatever we did. If the next hand was bad, we lost. If we lost all, Death came and took the cards away, clearing the table for someone else. I started life with a funeral, I could easily end it without one. The water was around my chest, and waves and sky made a white mist before my eyes. Now every muscle in me was slackened. I was asleep as I walked, the water lapping my throat and chin. If I opened my lips now I could let the sea flood in and fill me inside and out, till I floated away with the tide, gentle as kiss my hand.

The driftwood plank I'd seen before now floated into view. Now it was nearer and magnified in my water-level gaze. It swayed and bobbed gently and my body, feet lifting from the sand began to sway and bob in turn. All things in me within and without floated, the waves whispered in my ears and I began to swing with the great circle of the skyline. Comfort and ease filled my being.

Now, at last, there was Betsy, her face suspended half a foot above the water, smiling at me. If I stretched out my hand I could touch her, I thought, if my body were not so slack, so heavy.

"You coming out to meet me? That's famous."

"Betsy," I said, and stepped forward so the cool waves washed over my head and the water gurgled gently in my ears. Now the game was over and we were together.

There was a tremendous splashing and my poor body was seized by main force and dragged unwilling into the light.

"You bonehead!"

Why was Betsy speaking so angrily? I wondered, as I sank again, to the quiet depths.

And just as violently I rose again, the sky hard and blue over me. I was being tugged madly along, an iron grip on my hair. There was thrashing and spitting, pushing and pummelling and I landed like a hooked fish on the sand again.

My eyes opened. Betsy was there and I lay in her arms. I could see the ragged edge of her scarlet shift and her brown cheeks. If this was the end of the game, why had I played so long? I closed my eyes. She slapped my face. I opened them again.

"You rogue, to cheat me when I came back for you."

I rolled gently from her and crouched on my knees. There was the great hill, the curve of the bay, the woods and coming towards us slowly, Lady Alice and the Inventor. I turned to her.

"Are you real, Betsy?" I stretched out my hand to the plump, brown flesh showing where the shift was torn.

She slapped me, hard.

I leaped to my feet. She too.

"The ship?" I shouted.

"Went down. That fool Silver, to think he's my pappy. He laid the powder train wrong. Blew a hole in the ship's bottom off Spy Glass Hill. She went down in sight of shore."

"All were saved?"

She nodded. "All well. Tomorrow we vote."

"Ship or hut?" I asked.

She shook her head. "On whether we come down to Skeleton Island and string up my pappy or whether we don't."

"Is that true?"

She grinned. "Nanny won't let 'em do that. She's going to torment him a little bit longer."

I looked at her, red dress clinging to her long body and reached out. She slapped me. I sprang back. She pulled up the hem of her shift and knotted it between her legs.

"Best of three, eh Tom?" She leaped at me. I feinted, caught her as she slipped past, threw her over my hip and pinned her to the sand, where the waves ran over us. I fastened my lips on hers. She made to push me off.

"Best of three, I said," she mumbled.

"Suppose I lose?" I asked, and kissed her again.

193

As we rolled in the surf, I heard at a distance the voice of Lady Alice.

"Are they fighting, Mr Somerscale?"

"Reason would argue that they are not."

"There are some things to which the rule of reason must bow."

"Indeed, Lady Alice, can that be demonstrated?"

"Mr Somerscale, it can . . . come . . ."

Treasure Island
12 March 17—

Now my story's finished. More than I can say for the boat or the hut. We had so many votes on it that Old Wensleydale and Lady Alice invented a boat with a hut on top. Looks familiar to me and Dick Johnson reckons they got the idea from Genesis 6, verses 14–16.

The Spy Glass people did some voting too. Daniel and most of them wanted to help build the boat. Some others wanted to wait till it was finished then take it over. But what then? Some want to sail to Jamaica, some to Africa. And some want to stay here. Betsy says they reckon to have as much right to this island as anyone. I'll share any island with Betsy, even though she wants to settle every dispute between us with the best of three throws.

There's a deal of falling out, which keeps old Wilton-Stilton happy. But, says Dr Livesey, folk will fall out and no harm done, provided they don't cut each other's throats so Jim and he can't patch 'em up.

Mr Trelawney and Mr Argent go every day to Black Crag with Ned Barker. Those two used to watch Ned and the colliers shifting rocks. But now the colliers prefer fishing and gardening, so Squire and Argent have to do the humping while Ned oversees them. Nanny goes up there once a week to watch 'em. Says it makes her feel young again. But is the bar silver there? We only have Dick Johnson's word for it and he's not sure of aught, save that the Pearly Gates are waiting for him, thanks to little Tommy Carter.

I go for supper to North Inlet, first Sunday in every month. My name's carved on the back of that fourth chair. They're good company though on the quiet side. Dick has invited Squire and Mr Argent to come up and be forgiven, but they don't seem too eager.

6 September 17—
This month they reckon the rocks will be cleared and the ship launched. Dr L. says, "Take no chances," so I'm stowing this story in a rum cask and floating it off on the north-east current which they say washes the shores of Old England.

Any person finding this should go to the Admiral Benbow Inn and look under Master Hawkins' bed (provided the old lady's out). His story of Treasure Island lies there and, take my word for it, 'tis a rattling good yarn that ought to be published.

This island lies —° —' N —° —' W. The treasure, so Dick Johnson told me last Sunday, is buried under . . .

(Sea water must have got into the rum cask, for parts of the manuscript are indecipherable – R.L.)

'MAROON BOY
Robert Leeson

When Matthew Morten went to sea in 1568, he was a Bible-reading merchant's apprentice and the youngest hand aboard *The Golden Way*. He returned four years later with a reputation that included mutiny, raiding, and the nickname " 'Maroon Boy".

'Maroon is short for Cimaroon, a name given to escaped slaves who fought the Spanish in Panama and the English in Jamaica. It is known that Drake joined forces with the Cimaroons at one time, to harass the Spaniards: but where he was seeking gold, the Cimaroons wanted revenge on the white man.

Matthew Morten's motivations were even more complicated – though he didn't realise consciously what they were. Why he did what he did adds a fascinating moral dimension to this tale of swashbuckling adventure.

Bess

ROBERT LEESON

Bess Morten's flight from her overbearing guardian leads her to the New World in search of her brother Matthew. Determined and spirited, Bess has to fight for her right to independence, love, and to achieve the future she believes in.

This is an excellent adventure story and a sequel to *Maroon Boy*.

Bess is a character that 'ought to place her high among the fictional heroines with readers of today'.

British Book News

The White Horse

ROBERT LEESON

In this sequel to *'Maroon Boy* and *Bess*, Matt, Bess's son – the proud 'blackamoor' from New England – lands in Plymouth during the Civil War. He is haunted by dreams of a white stallion which comes to symbolise his quest – to avenge the wrong done to his mother and the murder of his father by the ruthless Sir Ralph Ferrers.

Matt's courage and uncompromising search for the truth takes him into many unexpected situations in this exciting adventure novel.

Complete in itself, *The White Horse* concludes a magnificent trilogy.

The Third Class Genie

ROBERT LEESON

Disasters were leading two nil on Alec's disaster-triumph scorecard, when he slipped into the vacant factory lot, locally known as the Tank. Ginger Wallace was hot on his heels, ready to destroy him, and Alec had escaped just in the nick of time. There were disasters awaiting him at home too, when he discovered that he would have to move out of his room and into the boxroom. And, of course, there was school . . .

But Alec's luck changed when he found a beer can that was still sealed, but obviously empty. Stranger still, when he held it up to his ear, he could hear a faint snoring . . . When Alec finally opened the mysterious can, something happened that gave triumphs a roaring and most unexpected lead.

A hilarious story for readers of ten upwards.

A Dark Horn Blowing

DAHLOV IPCAR

Far out across the sands stretching silver-white into the darkening bay, the cow was calling. That mourning, that sadness; it filled my whole soul with its sorrow. But there were words crying in the sound, and it was not the cow that spoke those words, but a small man with a horn standing by a long, black boat there at the edge of the tide. The cow's lowing became the dark horn blowing, and then it was too late – if ever I could have turned back I could no longer.

'Here is a remarkable piece of fantasy; haunting title, magical opening chapter – I can promise you the rest won't disappoint.' *Naomi Lewis*

GO WELL, STAY WELL
Toeckey Jones

Hamba kahle – Go well, stay well – is the Zulu phrase to wish a friend a safe journey, and one of the many things Candy learns from Becky. But had an accident not brought them together, they might never have met – never mind become such good friends. For although they live in the same South African city, their lifestyles could not be more different. While Candy's family have a large, comfortable house in the suburbs of Johannesburg, Becky lives in the black township of Soweto.

From the moment of their meeting, Candy and Becky realise just how difficult it is going to be to remain friends. The laws of apartheid that restrict meetings between blacks and whites put all number of obstacles in their way, and it is only their instinctive liking of one another that gives them the determination to fight for the right to share each other's company as equals.

Set in South Africa in 1976, this honest novel portrays the tensions and difficulties of that society and the feelings of many young people growing up there today.

The Darkangel
MEREDITH ANN PIERCE

The Darkangel was the most beautiful youth Aeriel had ever seen – a clear, icy, cold beauty with a radiance that faintly lit up the air. But Aeriel must destroy him before he takes a fourteenth and final bride and becomes a powerful vampire, capable of destroying the world. Can Aeriel resist the fatal allure of his splendour and breathtaking beauty or will the Darkangel destroy her?

The Darkangel is a compelling tale of mystery and romance set on the moon. It is a rich, inventive blend of myth, fantasy and superb storytelling.

'I found it was one of those books you do NOT put down until you have finished the last word . . .'
    Andre Norton

When Hitler Stole Pink Rabbit

Judith Kerr

Anna was only nine in 1933, too busy with her school work and her friends to take much notice of the posters of Adolf Hitler and the menacing swastikas plastered over Berlin. Being Jewish, she thought, was just something you were because your parents and grandparents were Jewish.

Suddenly, Anna's father was unaccountably missing. Shortly after, she and her brother were hurried out of Germany by their mother with alarming secrecy. Then began their rootless, wandering existence as refugees. Their life was often difficult and sad, but Anna soon discovered that all that really mattered was that the family was together.

An outstanding book for readers of ten upwards.